THE

SECOND

SUBSTANCE

THE

SECOND

SUBSTANCE

ANNE LARDEUX

translated by Pablo Strauss

COACH HOUSE BOOKS, TORONTO

Originally published in French by L'Oie de Cravan as *Les mauvais plis* by Anne Lardeux
Copyright © Anne Lardeux and L'Oie de Cravan, 2021
Translation copyright © Pablo Strauss, 2022

first edition

Coach House Books acknowledges the financial support of the Government of Canada. We are grateful for the generous assistance of the Canada Council for the Arts and the Ontario Arts Council. Coach House Books also acknowledges the support of the Government of Canada through the Canada Book Fund.

LIBRARY AND ARCHIVES CANADA CATALOGUING IN PUBLICATION

Title: The second substance / Anne Lardeux ; translated by Pablo Strauss.
Other titles: Mauvais plis. English
Names: Lardeux, Anne, author. | Strauss, Pablo, translator.
Description: Translation of: Les mauvais plis.
Identifiers: Canadiana (print) 20210386061 | Canadiana (ebook) 20210386126 | ISBN 9781552454398 (softcover) | ISBN 9781770567092 (PDF) | ISBN 9781770567085 (EPUB)
Classification: LCC PS8623.A7467 M3813 2022 | DDC C843/.6—dc23

The Second Substsance is available as an ebook: ISBN 978 1 77056 708 5 (EPUB), ISBN 978 1 77056 709 2 (PDF)

Purchase of the print version of this book entitles you to a free digital copy. To claim your ebook of this title, please email sales@chbooks.com with proof of purchase. (Coach House Books reserves the right to terminate the free digital download offer at any time.)

To the women brought together by Kabane 77

'Then there are those over whom the events and opportunities of the everyday world wash over. There is rarely, in this second type, any easy kind of absorption. There is only a visible evidence of having been made of a different substance, one that repels. Also, from them, it is almost impossible to give to the world what it will welcome or reward. For how does this second type hold their arms? Across their chest? Behind their back? And how do they find food to eat and then prepare this food? And how do they receive a check or endorse it? And what also of the difficulties of love or being loved, its expansiveness, the way it is used for markets and indentured moods?

'And what is this second substance? And how does it come to have as one of its qualities the resistance of the world as it is?'

– Anne Boyer, 'At Least Two Types of People'

A large cast of characters. And in the middle,
like the hub of a wheel,
Antonia, a growing girl. She'll disappear.
Nothing bad will become of her. Leaving was her choice.
Her departure is hard to explain, but vital.
Her father, a blind potter,
washed up on these backroads.
No one knows how,
maybe he just stopped rolling.
His name is Peter.
There's the girl who eats cereal,
chips, beer, and cheese curds.
Her plan: meet people, connect,
sleep with them when it's right.
She has no name.
She's in a group, working on an invention,
some martial technique,
some new form of life.
Then there's Mona. The lengths she'll go to.
She's impressive, delirious, who really knows?
An Old Man tans hides, another brings hallucinations.
There are children. And off on his own,
a sullen teen.
A policewoman
who has ceased to uphold the Law.
A girl whose name sounds like the word 'frenetic'
come to give history a shove toward direct action.
At the Station, a community crystallizes,
a group that exists now only in scattered memories.
Movement is a form of flight,
and resistance.

The asphalt no longer softens in the heat. Like the ageing skin on the back of a hand, it fissures into a diamond pattern broken only by inoffensive, stubborn bumps.

The ground is rising up, disarming the road. The parched earth itself wants to take flight. The withered trees on either side have not caught fire, not tonight, though the bone-dry air is abuzz, primed for a great blaze. Throughout this world, revolt is welling up and creeping in on false respite.

Two women, one still a girl, the other, well, it's hard to say, sweep a deserted stretch of road. Intently they gather up and flick away the debris that has chipped off the blacktop. The shorter one kneels, palming the surface. The taller one stretches out on her stomach with an ear to the hot asphalt. The ground takes her weight; she abandons herself to it.

Later, when both have gotten to their feet, they stand with hands on hips in an evening light that traces the contours of a hope they measure out by eye. This evening is like every other, no spark to ignite the Revolution, just another evening leading tediously to another day.

'Well, that's that,' says the woman.

The girl doesn't respond. She answers to the name *Antonia*. The woman? It's complicated, maybe political, but there's no name we can give her that she would accept.

GROUNDS AND ARGUMENTS

ANTONIA THE RUNAWAY

I ran away because I couldn't figure out what else to do.

I wasn't after anything in particular. But I wanted to experience something.

I ended up on the road. There isn't really more to it. It's not like I've run away from everyone.

THE GIRL WITH NO NAME

I was searching for moments of radical autonomy and that made me attach myself to others. Nameless relationships became my direct action. I make my way hither and yon and touch them one and all. There is skin, coarse or smooth, and breathing. Hair and calloused feet, necks and asses, stiff cocks, wet pussies, young and old and neither quite. I am errant and unproductive and my freedom is my burden to bear.

THE TRIGGERING EVENT

In her parents' living room, The Girl With No Name sits on the edge of a chair near the door, toying with the idea of running away. She who is usually so carefully made up has grown greasy-haired and bloated on this family visit. She knits. At her feet, a small girl plays with action figures, conjuring up their tragic human fates in a terrible whisper.

'Get your carts! Saddle your horses. I'm gonna kill you! Oh? No, no! Take pity … Take shelter, my love. Quick! Oh, my king. Aaarrrgh. Take your sash, to heal my wound. It's too late. He's dying. Bring a glass of water and a knife. I'll raise an army of urchins, save my dying people!'

The young woman knitting gets drawn into the story of the campaign being waged on the carpet. With her knitting on her knee, she drifts into a reverie. *There is water. She is at first on the shore, then in a grassy valley. The wind's strange rustling grows louder. A riotous horde tramples by. Many are the wounded. The oozing bandages wrapped around their heads give no sense whether they've been wounded in their ears or their teeth. Some hold up crutchless comrades. The women carry children and dirty bundles. An old woman offers her a hunk of bread. It's hard as rock. The crowd is driven forward by a yellow horse that towers over them like a monument, pulling a sleigh piled high with bundles and housewares.*

The Girl With No Name watches this precarious load pass her by without moving, and amid the great clanging of iron, untempered by the slightest mumble or laugh, she meets the gaze of a minuscule, hollow-eyed girl. The child's head has slipped between two chair legs, which she clasps in her tiny hands. As soon as she appears she is gone, pushed along by the crowd.

Bringing up the rear of this long march are animals that have long ceased to dream of freedom or conceive a life independent of humans. Three pigs, one goat, two cows, one limping turkey. She watches the starveling horde until it disappears.

When silence settles and even the echoes of their advance have faded to nothing, she kneels like a huntress to read the tracks this motley troupe left behind. No prints in this soft clay, just a formless mess that offers no clue about this migration or its urgency.

Left alone in the strong winter wind, she wonders what to make of it all.

Her newfound concentration is sharp as a blade, but tender. The Girl With No Name sets out down the road, walking through fields, ignoring the long grass that scrapes her legs. She steps over pipelines and train tracks, searching for the suburban patchwork and the chipped concrete of deserted tunnels. Leaving fear behind, she sets forth to receive the waves of the world.

THE CRACKLE OF DOUBT

I place the tape recorder on the desk in front of me and press STOP/EJECT. The door opens, with the muffled *thwock* of plastic and metal springs. I put in a blank tape, shut the cassette door and, with my two index fingers, press the red REC and black PLAY buttons down together. Tape rolls.

> *I'm very afraid.*
> *I have moments of horrible anguish, when I tell myself I'll never make it.*
> *And it's true ... I might not make it, but I'm going to keep trying anyway.*
> (Sigh)
> *Anyway, that's it. Bye.*

I press STOP. Consider REWIND, to take another listen. I'm reading the message Delphine Seyrig recorded and sent to her son when she was called to New York for a role.

I collect missives of doubt and discouragement, feelings of failure. I don't really know why – to ward off my fears, perhaps? Or embrace my impending failures?

I stand to look at myself in the mirror. Turn my head to glimpse my profile, and that's when I see him through the window. No longer in a private space, I get down on all fours. *Shit! What's he doing here?* He finishes locking his bike to the metal grille and pushes on the main door. *What? No!* He rings the bell. *But why?* He's persistent. Maybe he didn't see me? It seems hard to believe.

I crawl over to the hallway to step away from the window, but when he rings a third time, longer now, I do as I've been taught. *Okay, open the door, like a grownup.*

We chat. The man was just passing by. I offer him a glass of water. He leaves. I close the door, whisper an annoyed *Goodbye.* Feeling crushed, I turn off my computer without saving and sit down on the bed. I have no idea what structure even looks like, can't say for sure I'd recognize one if it slapped me in the face. I have no clear sense of where I'm going or where I might feel better.

I take off my jeans and panties and slide under the quilt. I want to masturbate, to forget, but with my head full of such brittle words I can't loosen up or get wet. Before losing heart I drift off to sleep. Between my legs I lay my hands, redundant now to all lubricious plans.

We now join our story, already in progress.

APRIL 21

We live – four guys, two girls – in an abandoned, repurposed Shell station. We live here, under the burnt-out light of a totem of industry, the blazoned fossil of conquest lost. That's where she found us.

At first she kept her distance. Kicked up dust in the no-man's-land next to our lot. There were rake handles and other tools sticking out of the bed of her pickup. She'd parked sideways in a field. Her truck was her home base.

We thought nothing of it. Our minds were blank as a dog scratching its ear, staring out at the horizon. She seemed so natural, invisible, fully part of some ambient reality. Then she sidled over and our door opened and that reality slipped in with her. Her body was all ropy muscle and her tan was leathery from working outside, and she left me feeling woozy. I didn't at first understand what she was doing to me. She was just there. Keen. I sat there finishing my cereal. I could sense danger and I could feel myself running headlong toward it.

She lived on a stretch known as Précieux-Sang. A rundown farm with a junkyard out front on a backroad in the outskirts of Bécancour County, an ailing expanse of highway and river-front, struggling factories, dairy farms and hog farms and grain silos and a decommissioned nuclear power plant waiting to be dismantled and a microbrewery on the riverbank. This countryside still eludes human dominion but is pushed ever further out by soulless practicalities, a land of clapboard, condensed milk, and clover honey.

Mona does some sort of landscaping. She drives around in her truck with her sullen teenaged son, who helps her out in the summer. Her other, younger kids appear so rarely we forget all about them. They have cavity-ridden smiles and wiry muscles, like feral prairie dogs.

Mona's routine is set: beer day and night, cheese curds at five in the morning, a hot dog when the party gets rolling. Like an animal, she showed up in our yard and didn't even have to bare her teeth to make off with our alpha male. I still fear her a little, though she doesn't know I know that she could have taken any of our men without a fight. To process my confusion I'm stuffing my face with the staples of comfort: milk, cereal, muffins, chips, beer – day or night, whatever. I'm on some sort of vacation, burning through the last of my savings. There's always time for fasting; that time is always later.

Mona has other appetites. She expects nothing from life but what she's willing to take. Comes and goes at will, takes what she wants, leaves when she's had enough. She's beautiful but spurned by the villagers. They stare uncomprehendingly, lacking the imagination to do anything but mock her for the things she doesn't have: above-ground pool, giant grill on a teak deck, friends to gather round the table, A/C to cool them off. They call her backroads trash and cross the road to avoid her belligerent stare – it's piercing by day, liquid by night, murderous around the clock. She at once disgusts and fascinates them. And me? Mona kills me dead.

All that time we thought we were at our place, we were really at his place...

One night a noise wakes me. Faint – maybe a dog? I turn over in the hope of getting back to sleep. But it's hot in the room and the sound is insistent and I don't. Finally I sit up with a start and a racing heart, on high alert. No doubt about it, there's someone downstairs. Claire is sleeping beside me, I give her a shake. She turns over and mumbles something. I whisper the alarm and see her eyes widen in the dark. She stares at the ceiling, the better to hear and identify the noise. A chair is being pulled out. She sits up and squeezes my arm. I look for a weapon, find a stick but drop it and instead pick up one of the empties that litter the floor. I turn it around – there, a weapon.

Claire wakes up the guys spooning on the mattress beside us, bodies exhausted from incessant exploration. In this crudely furnished attic we sleep on mattresses chucked on the ground, with strung-up sheets our only privacy. Now we go down the stairs in a close-knit group, armed with flashlights and whatever we have managed to lay hands on. We find him sitting at the table. He is hirsute and dishevelled, like a deer caught in our headlights. He's come home. In the flickering light of our inept settlement, he demands a drink.

By squatting his home we've become part of his story.

The Old Man is an outcast. The village leaves him be when he wanders in from the woods and stays in the abandoned gas station. He's a vaguely disconcerting alcoholic vagabond. The townsfolk keep their distance. I got caught in his snare.

Mathieu is on a video call with his mom, lying on the bed with his laptop on his stomach. He has pulled the curtain. I'm hiding behind my book on the next mattress over.

His raspy-voiced mother is nervously asking the usual questions. He tries to ease the tension by telling her about his walks in the woods, how you can feel spring coming in the lengthening days. His soil tests, the lab he's setting up in a shed. Even over the digital distance, you can feel her not listening. She asks no questions and punctuates her son's descriptions with little dry *Oh*s that drop like small disapproving stones into a line marking a path to somewhere else.

Mathieu can tell. 'What about you? How are you?' he asks. His mom lights up another smoke and taps her lighter on the table I imagine her sitting at. I put down my book and listen in.

She doesn't like to complain but still. They've been harassing her for weeks. A collection agency. She repeats its name to her incredulous son and spells it out as well: 'S' as in 'servitude,' 'e' as in 'enslaved,' 'r' as in 'responsibility,' 'f' as in 'failure.' Silence. M. gets up and crosses over to my side of the curtain. He swivels between the computer screen he's holding at a distance from his face and me, lying flabbergasted on my bed.

'If you don't call back and make a deal, they're going to repossess my car. Take everything I own. I just know it! They're scum! But it's fine if you don't … I'll just pay it myself.'

The son snaps around, as if thrown back by a slap in the face, and strides across the attic in confusion.

'They're just trying to intimidate you. We're going to get organized, but first you have to stop answering their calls, okay? That's the first thing. You can't give in to them. Do you get it?'

Does she? It's hard to say: she's too afraid to stop and think or take a breath, so she keeps shoving the same words into the pigeonhole of his guilt.

'Fine, I'll just pay it. I'm your mother, after all.'

'Jesus, Mom! That doesn't help me. It's the opposite! If you pay, it'll undo all our work, everything I'm trying to do with this corrupt system. Why can't you understand?'

But Mathieu's mother wasn't raised that way. Him neither, for that matter, but he changed. In his mother's book, *a debt's a debt*. She'd let herself be drawn and quartered to pay back what her son owes.

Untenable sacrifice. *O mother. O mercy. O thank you.*

APRIL 29

This morning Mathieu packed his bag and I dropped him off at the on-ramp to Highway 55. He's on his way back to Montreal. He's bummed. It's cold.

'I just gotta fix this one thing, then I'll be back. Take care!'

'You too. Give us a call.'

On my way back to the Station, I try to hold on to the warmth of our embrace, but his absence left an emptiness that chills me.

We've been here for months now. Nothing is certain. Are we exhausted from the months of freezing cold, or just bored and lacking in purpose? It's been a long winter, for sure, and it's only now letting up a little. Just three of us left now – four if you count the Old Man, who has stopped going out into the woods.

In these lengthening days we walk through the fields, lazily chasing the crows pecking at half-frozen worms in the earth.

We march like prisoners, trying to burn off excess energy. *Where is a life free from the strictures of routine, beating free and unthinking like wings, fulfilling our every need?*

MAY 1

So many anxious nights when sleep plays hard to get, so many hours with the same nagging questions in our heads: How can we change the course of the things and beings that threaten us, without killing them? How to produce some vital substance – discourse, images, currency, matter, energy, sex – without dispossessing ourselves?

Are we at war in the same way our enemies are? Can the substance to fuel our struggle be produced? Can a deep kiss be a political act? What forces can our imaginations conjure up? Which tensions sustain our struggle, and which ones pull us away from it?

Skeptically we twirl our cold spaghetti and stub out our cigarettes right on our plates. We're exhausted by the constant need for engineering, doubts mushrooming in the loam of our fallow desires.

As the meaning and purpose of our actions dissipates, a nagging guilt seeps in. The roof that shelters us flaps in the wind. Inside we've stopped picking up what falls to the ground: empty bottles, full ashtrays, clean and dirty dishes in one pile, opposites thrown in together, nothing seems to matter anymore. I grieve for our tired, numb bodies that so rarely now find their way to arousal.

I'm trying to keep a regular journal of the Station, to leave at least some trace of our endeavours. And I do, through thick and thin. After periods of short entries, weeks and months gapped like bad teeth, my thoughts surge in waves, lucid and ecstatic at their crest but worn and frayed by anxiety in the depths of their troughs. The momentum from manic-depressive peaks speeds me through the valleys.

When the burnt-out light of our totem becomes too oppressive, and we've run out of the milk and beer of human comfort, I go to the City. One night on the north side I see people passing through a narrow gap in the chain-link fence along the railroad tracks, sliding into a small field they are working to protect. A woman at this break in the fence thanks people for coming, as if ushering them into her living room. It's cold and looks like rain is on the way. The men have beards, thick flannel shirts, and toques; the women, well, it's more complicated but they've found ways to be pretty in the cold. All gather together here after a manner, but only the ones who know each other touch.

I want to touch the skin of the ones who have stopped seeking out human contact, I want to be seen by the ones the light does not find. I want to find openings, breaks in the fence.

I GOT THIS

I'm not even sure I can tell this story. And I'm not saying that because I'm looking for reassurance.

I'm a lost seventies girl in an accelerating world, running like a hamster on a wheel, writing this book by flashlight, taking one dimly lit step at a time. I describe what I see, with no sense of a whole and no clear idea where I've been. I think with my feet.

H. encourages me to be generous. *Don't hold back, say what needs to be said.* What I hear is: *carry the weight, do the work. If you clear a path, go there. Put yourself out there.* And I believe her. She trusts me and I believe in this trust, and in belief begins one more responsibility on top of those I bear as a mother and daughter and loyal friend: to write down this fucking story, and to work in enough sex so people can at least get off a little.

So yeah, I guess I've got this.

Sex isn't incidental, though.
Not a sideline in this story.
It's the driving force thereof.

JUNE 2

I'm getting down to work. One night I slip into the trapper's bed in the storeroom off the kitchen. For a long time I stay still, like a plank. I slow my breathing to internalize the rhythm of his. His old skin is coarse, I know without touching it. There are the waves he emits, a force of attraction. His old body is shy, so when a long time has passed and he still has not moved, I do. My hand moves over my own body first, breasts and stomach and hipbones. It slides under the covers, shimmies up onto his arms – hair, mass, a warm dense matter made of and for work. His breathing grows heavier, but still he does not move. My hand slides over his broad chest and then down lower, to his navel and pubic hair and then his cock that has begun to stir. I squeeze it in my hand, stroke him off, palm his balls, and then my mouth joins my hand, nuzzles up and in we go. I crawl back up to kiss him, my tongue is melting in his mouth, I lose myself down his throat. I crouch on him, his cock now standing at attention, *swing baby, swing,* and now he lets himself join in, grabs my thighs. And he flips me over, again and again, and under his weight, I moan.

JUNE 6

I go to the attic to look for Claire. She's spread out on the mattress reading Virginia Woolf. We always say it in a lupine howl, '*WOOOOOOLF.*' Raring for a fight, I do a two-footed leap onto the bed, vault Virgie into the air, and jump around with one foot on either side of her body. She doesn't react. I jump down off the bed. A ray of sun exposes the dust, spinning like an infinite number of small planets. I lap them up, punch the air with my arms, *C'mon, put 'em up, show me what you got!* I bend my knees, ready to fight. My games aren't fun anymore, her heart's not in it. She rolls over onto her stomach. I pick up my book. Fine.

The smell of alcohol has been slowly infusing the Station since we moved in. It stinks like a distillery barrel.

JUNE 10

One morning Mona shows up in our yard. She leans on her pickup, haughty, maniacal. I go out in my pyjamas. Low-hanging sky, a day full of promise. I want to eat my cereal but don't dare while she's here. So I sit on the porch, fakebusy, keeping an eye on her. She's smoking and I'm waiting for her to flick her butt in my direction, but instead she grinds it out with her boot.

'I need you.'

I play dumb.

'It's the flower festival Monday and I'm super busy. I need you to give us a hand.'

I pull on the T-shirt that I cropped too short and look up at the sky. Fine. Inside, the Old Man is tapping on the thin wood window frame: rattling the bug screens, staring out at me. I turn my head. He whistles, sharp as an axe, as if to call me out for violating the Trapper's Code. I'm his property now. He tans my hide like a precious commodity. His hands know the work. The truck door bangs shut; she leaves. I turn my back to the Old Man.

Claire wants to leave, her mind's made up, I know there's nothing I can do. I don't want her to go, but I still help her gather her things and pack her bag. I come to terms with her leaving and drop her off at the Nicolet bus depot.

We park across from the Police Academy. We're early, so we lean on the hood of the car and I watch Claire perform the Smoker's Shuffle that I do love so. She takes her pack from her shirt pocket, pinches her thumb and index finger to bring it to her lips, sucks it into her mouth with a little movement, and then clenches it between her teeth so she can talk at the same time.

'Where's my goddamn lighter?'

Her hands pat down various parts of her body in search of that small lump, and there it is, in her back pocket. Fingers make shelter for flame, and I add my two hands as a windbreak, and here's a cherry and a soft crackling. She inhales, then blows smoke up toward the sky. It's a moment of joy, the same series of movements in perpetual rotation. I look at her avidly, to soak up her presence, drink it in until I'm sated. I'd like to say something meaningful. Nothing comes. She points at the school across from us and gestures with her chin, *look*.

A battalion of recruits has assembled on the basketball court. Each body wears a T-shirt and blue shorts. A man screams orders. The silhouettes seem uncertain and try to follow the plan. They hold arms out here and there, and little by little their bodies align with one another, hands and arms nearly touching, forming a square. In the background their captain alternates between blowing his whistle and yelling incomprehensibly. Bodies bend, heels to asses, and then leap up in a single bound, arms reaching for the sky again, folded over in a crouch on the ground, extended to the heavens. A blast of the whistle: they reluctantly stop, and ears prick up toward the commanding officer, before turning around again. An attempt to move the troop falters … Panicked heads toggle from left to right in an attempt to understand. Distances are confusing: in some spots the recruits are close together and elsewhere the space seems to stretch on forever. The man with the whistle is losing his shit. He throws it to the ground and crosses his arms in ominous silence. Discreetly the silhouettes attempt to regain what might pass for a dignified formation.

Even with hearts wrenched by our imminent separation, we chuckle at the pointless manoeuvres of these obedient trainees. In the row closest to us a woman pulls up her socks and, as if she has heard us, turns to us, her face a closed book. Claire gives her a little wave goodbye.

But the bus is here. I pull the bags from the car and pass them to Claire, who stubs out her smoke. She takes me by the shoulder and gives me a cursory hug. *C'mon, you know where to find me.* I watch her set off into the distance.

Then it's back to the Station. One fewer woman here now.

Our group is changing, but my mind is elsewhere. People come and people go.

All my energy goes into my play with the Old Man, who is gracious enough to be honoured by my attentions. His tan skin clashes with my own, so white. He darkens me.

THE SALAMANDER

I'm writing this book and I find myself shaking. An uncontrollable trembling seizes me, knocks me down. I seek out the ground, its inevitability. I should smack it with my palm to acknowledge my fall and then get up like a good judoka. Except I don't get up.

The people around me spring into action. They are concerned, want to come to my aid. I sit like a rag doll in the midst of this excitement. My breathing becomes regular, I finally feel calm. The ground holds steady – thanks, ground.

My skirt hitched up a little when I fell. It's almost nothing, a tiny gap in the fabric in the middle of my thighs. Not big, but I can feel it through my tights, the touch of cool air in a place normally covered. I tell myself, *This is the start of something* – an uprising, some kind of strike? I'm the spark of a walkout. I'm the tight-wound rapture of 'the girls' right before all the machines in the great workshop grind to a halt. A silence descends, thrumming, on the immobilized line, the great idle behemoth stripped of its trembling forward motion, of its parts, of production itself; pulsing hands shoved deep into the pockets of smocks that the girls are trying to keep still, gloves dropped at their feet, the beating of their hearts in their throats.

I may be on my own – with no team, no colleagues, no work per se – but I'm running this show, telling this story. I focus on my hiked-up skirt and exposed thighs, owning my undutiful desire to not pull it back down and to paralyze the workshop: yank off my underwear, pop out my breasts, get down on all fours so they shake above the ground as I shriek unapologetically or yell whatever comes to mind, whatever isn't pretty.

'Beauty won't always be enough for us,' said an angry woman on the radio the other day, a writer. No better the pitiless bright lights that expose us, scorching the earth even unto this last story that we've hidden under that rock, like a marvellous salamander in the depths of the night. Let us hide away the books that need to be written, and if we must flee let us sew their pages to the linings of our tattered gowns.

LINES ON THE FLOOR

The school gym is empty. The principal, a short man, does a quick walk-through to pace out the dimensions. Something is clearly wrong. A policewoman walks in, hand on holster. She takes in the naked, brightly lit space. It smells of warmth. She checks out what she has identified as the problem: a woman sitting on a bench beside the basketball hoop. Her head rests in her hands, then rises to the heavens and back into her hands in an attitude somewhere between threat and supplication.

The harnessed officer hesitates between the two – stormy tearful woman, school principal – but neither sees her, so she makes her way to centre court and takes up a position in the big red circle with her arms crossed. Only then does the principal notice her. He walks over and stops at the edge of the large circumference.

'Do we have a problem?' she asks, looking him up and down, her posture ramrod straight.

He looks at her and hesitates. His principal's reflexes momentarily bristle, but without a fuss he relaxes. Arms and head, torso and knees, all together the whole edifice collapses. He crumples onto the waxed gym floor at the policewoman's feet. His entire career is spread out on his defeated face: decades of memos and reports and the minutes of meetings both monthly and annual general, staff schedules and Excel files recording each and every action and reaction, the retreat of common sense and pedagogy. He has patched the cracks with prescription drugs and alcohol. He's on his knees now, head down, though he raises it along with the narrow-framed pattern-armed glasses that have slipped down his nose.

Almost tenderly, he begins.

'She sent the child out of her classroom – not long, just long enough to get the message across, I guess. She closed the classroom door. But when she came back to get him, the kid wasn't there. Just ten minutes later! No more. He was gone! You know how they are …'

And here now comes the woman, rushing over with the look of one who will never give in.

'It wasn't ten minutes. I only left him unsupervised five minutes!'

The officer stares at her without moving from her circle. The two authority figures size each other up.

I wonder, the policewoman thinks, *what the difference is between us. Not much … nothing really. I could tell her to go get changed, put on a uniform. You'll see how the kids snap into line.'*

Their face-to-face is interrupted by the crackling walkie-talkie at her hip. The officer looks away from the teacher, then puts it to her mouth to answer. Another woman arrives, runs over, yells out. Her cries hit home, come from the heart: she's the mother. The officer pivots on the court, the walkie-talkie falls to her feet and does not turn back on for more. The Order of Things pivots, savagery comes out from the shadows, failing to respect the lines marked on the court.

The kid didn't get far. He went home. The policewoman hung up the radio call and shut the hatch on her feelings, sealed tight by the Order of Things.

People think nothing is happening, but that's not it. More like nothing that's happening directly affects us, here, and we stay dry, here, out of reach of the splashes of horror. Our reality, packed hard like a snowbank in front of a parking lot, remains unbroken. But the war isn't over. The war is ongoing, perpetual, sucking the life from us, pulverizing everything in its path. We aren't ankle-deep in in a toxic mix of saltwater and marine fuel, drowning in an overloaded Zodiac in a hostile, starless night. We aren't murdered or missing Indigenous women and girls, we aren't dying in some hospital while the nurses insult us and the guards yell at us. Where we live, the credit cards are loaded for perpetuity and strangers are kept at a distance. And in the midst of all we do not know, something sometimes cracks and ruptures, admitting the possibility of love or true despair that will soak us like the water in the bottom of a boat. O *Captain, this crossing.*

The frame fades to black in an iris shot,
like in a Truffaut film, or maybe something more handmade like Olivier Godin.

THE POLICEWOMAN'S CONFESSION

I'm a police officer. A police*woman*. I wear blue slacks that hug my pelvis and make my ass look big. I wear a baseball cap with my ponytail threaded through, the way you dress up dolls.

I wanted to approach men. I wanted to approach men without their consent. This is the way I found. That moment on the road when I walk over to the car at the stop sign at the bottom of the hill, hand on holster, and the window rolls down and I see the men's faces, drawn with concern over their misdemeanour. I love their diligence, the way their anxious hands fumble for their cards.

I scan the horizon. I have all the time in the world. Everyone is in position, this moment can't be taken back. I take out my pad, note the infraction and its penalty. My colleague punches it into the system, the blue screen reflecting on his forehead scrunched up with concentration. Points are flying, tickets stacking up.

Cool and collected, I amble over to the offending vehicle. Inside, someone is watching me in the rear-view, trying to figure out whether something is going to happen to him. I reach out my left hand with the ticket held out for the offending driver and lean my right elbow on the roof.

I stare down their feelings, their anger and apathy and occasional attempts to seduce or resist. I derive pleasure from the way their faces stare up at me, like children, and with my cop's gloves I dream of caressing their chins, pulling them toward me as I lean in to kiss their penitent mouths.

I wanted to approach men – what better way than joining the police? I wanted to try on their panoply of armour, mirror their movements, feel that self-satisfaction that stretches their uniforms tight and fuels their feeling of omnipotence. It's not enough to be with them; I want to *be them*. I'm not Ken's wife; I *am* Ken, and that drives them mad. But I have to be more than a reassuring presence, so they'll invite me to join in their backseat bacchanals. I want to guide their hands as they jerk off with their mouths full. I want to be one of them, for them to no longer fear me; I want to connect, but not be some random pussy they fuck blind. I want to walk beside them, alongside them toward the cars parked at the bottom of the hill. Spread bodies out on the hoods, shake up their handcuffed bodies, separate the stinking bodies and gather up the limp ones and drag away the ones we've banged up. I want to bask in their absolute trust.

I don't know what I'm looking for, exactly. Is my investigation still an open case? Maybe I just need to harness my anger for this army, refuse to put my weakness in bondage. But I see all too clearly what these men are up to. C'mon. I'm not blind to the fatality swelling in their ranks. It's insane, a hellish resentment, a bottomless well.

And that's how I got up one fine morning and put on a clean shirt and signed up for the Quebec Police Academy in Nicolet. The year was 2001. I became a policewoman.

'It's not hard. What I'm asking. I just hate doing it.'

'Doing what?'

'Folding paper flowers for the festival. Helping the day-camp kids.'

'Hmmm … pffft … I don't really have a choice, I guess?'

'That's right! It's easy, you'll see.'

The sullen teen opens the door and gets out of the truck so the Girl with No Name can sit between him and his mom. She scoots over, he gets in, the door bangs shut. The cab smells like warm dust and leaking oil. Mona starts the car and the Girl with No Name's thighs stick to the clammy plastic seat. A rumbling shakes through them and her knee touches the sullen teen's. He's listening to music in his headphones, casually nodding his head to a rhythm he can't hold. She catches his eye in the rear-view mirror and they make contact in the reflection, and when the car turns they seek each other out and their knees brush against each other. Mona pulls into the parking lot of the Bécancour Arena. She points at a small cluster of kids by the door.

'You're working with them. We're off to Gentilly.'

The Girl With No Name regretfully leaves behind her shelter and the boy's deep eyes and downy leg hairs. He gets out to let her climb down and then jumps back in. The truck trundles off toward other obligations.

The kids from the day camp are already there, lined up in the shade of the arena's awning. Baseball caps, backpacks, lunchboxes, fluorescent T-shirts: it's another day at the office for these uniformed children. She takes her place in this lineup of seasonal workers, though she lacks the right outfit and tools of the trade. She wants a smoke but the pack of Players sits forgotten on the kitchen table. She doesn't even have change for a French Vanilla coffee from the machine in the lobby. The kids give her funny looks. She stays there, so silent no one dares talk to her. The slow passage of time eventually appeases them. She sits cross-legged and scratches the ground with a stick. They keep their cool, standing stoically before the uncertainty of this new day of camp. She glances furtively around and finds that some of the kids aren't actually that young. Especially the tall girl over there who has given up her place in line and is coming over to sit with her.

'Hey! You here for the camp?'

The Girl With No Name stutters out, 'Yeah, no, just help-ing out with the flowers for the parade. You?'

The girl looks down nervously from under her long bangs.

'No, I'm doing an internship, as a counsellor.'

With two hands she parts the curtain of her hair and, looking square in the Girl With No Name's eyes, as if to impress upon her the seriousness of the matter at hand, she says, 'I'm Antonia.'

JUNE 20

In the arena there's a gym and I'm there with the kids, all of us waiting for something to happen. A young woman shows up, finally. Her skin is carotene-tan, her eyebrows so plucked they do not rise to ask what I am doing here. So I stand up instead.

'I'm here for the paper flowers. Mona sent me ...'

The kids tuck this information away in their lunch boxes, like a snack. The woman tosses her straight blond hair back and offers me a bony manicured hand.

'I'm Canella.'

As she says her name, so soft and blond, her eyebrows drop in a slow, almost tender movement. She tilts her head toward her slender shoulder, and her hand travels up to caress my cheek with a quizzical *How are you?* I turn my mouth toward her palm and give her an open-mouthed kiss, saying, 'Good, now that you're here,' which isn't untrue. The kids have stood up. The young intern gives me back my stick, adjusts her shorts, which are riding up her ass, and pulls up her socks. The gym smells like warm rubber and athlete's foot. Folding tables line the wall. Banks of fluorescent tubes project a game-day light, but there are no balls to suggest we might play, and no one here is fooled anyway, they just keep standing there with their packs on their backs.

Canella is unfazed. Her lithe body effortlessly inhabits another sphere where efficiency reigns, far above our discontent. While we're still milling around the centre of the gym, she has already unfolded two tables, set out the materials — scissors, glue, crepe paper — and even made a model.

'See! It's easy. For the Natural Gas float we'll need 1,400 whites, 1,250 blues, 600 greys, and 500 browns. Then we'll see for the rest. Hop to it!'

She brushes against me, short shorts clinging to her Barbie-doll ass, and I belong to her, *Canella won't you be my girl, give me a kiss, c'mon.* In her V-neck, everything is tucked tight and cushiony soft, snug in those glued-on shorts, and there's her blond arm hair that escaped the aesthetician's laser eye, *Canella, my little dumpling, slides her tongue into my mouth, it's more than I'd dare hope for, and then she takes over, rubbing my pussy through my jeans, her manicured hands caressing the soft mounds in the tight fabric. And I swell, and I melt. But Canella is already off on her way, off to her Corvette to run an errand for her baaabe who's running low on protein powder.* I let out a sigh in the middle of the gym. Looking around, I no longer see childlike stares but instead tiny workers engrossed in their task. I am flushed red and hot. I join them.

We start folding. With small hands used to busywork, my campmates prove more dextrous and productive than I am. I find myself swept up by the repetitive movements, and soon I am elsewhere. *I walk over to the edge of a lake, in a buzzing of flies. Pull my shorts and panties down, down to my ankles, pull my T-shirt over my head. I feel the warm air in my navel and armpits and pussy and spread my legs to help it along. I go down deep down into the oily dark water, it isn't cold, I open up, I lean face-down over the lake, the tips of my nipples brush the water's surface and the word 'tit' comes to mind; I push it back but still I feel my nipples getting hard. I lie there, rubbing and circling myself with lake water. And now the lake's between my legs.*

Hours go by and after a while I no longer see the children's hands buried under the rustling piles of coloured crepe paper we're supposed to be folding. I've come back down to earth, can no longer launch out into unexplored waters. I decide to run off and save someone. The young intern looks at me and I wonder whether, all things considered, at some point before we wear our hands down to the bone with this all folding, I can ask, 'Want to get out of here?'

Antonia hides her unfinished flower under the table, grabs her lunchbox and backpack, puts her cap back on and, in her oversized Camp Marmoset T-shirt, she beats me to the door. No doubt about it: she's the leader, I'm the follower.

We walk through the arena parking lot and take the main street along the river, passing a Monster Gym that clearly wasn't built to last. We cross the strip mall parking lot, gravitating toward the purple fluorescent lights like moths to a flame, and peer through the window. The low-ceilinged rectangular room is full of machines with horns and pedals, or narrow benches piled with giant rings made of dense materials. A few buff dudes are lifting weights in front of a mirror that covers the back wall. They face us. Antonia elbows me as her chin points toward the room's right side. Canella, leaning against a stationary bike, seems a million miles away from the arena and its mountains of crepe paper. Antonia grabs my wrist and pulls, we have to go, *I can't let her see me.* A woman gets out of her car and walks toward the door, carrying a sports bag and nursing a scowl. She shoulders me out of the way and disappears under the fluorescent lights. Antonia looks at me sideways.

'She's a policewoman.'

We make our way along the main road. The houses are so close we could touch them, some fading and cracking in original cladding and others cruelly re-sided in beige vinyl and still others fake-old-timey. A man is pulling weeds in his flowerbeds. He stops and looks at us, face opaque as a moonless night. Antonia leads the way along the narrow sidewalk, with her hands on the straps of her knapsack, holding it tight to her back. The sidewalk disappears, the shoulder widens, the houses have receded behind less well-kept yards where leisure products are scattered in with domestic tools. A trampoline, a rusty harrow, a doghouse whose resident barks and yanks at his chain. An upside-down kids' pedal tractor. Not a living soul can be seen around the deserted above-ground pools. Though summer's just beginning, everything is already yellow, the previous months' snow brutally melted in a constant heat that both soothes and alarms us.

Antonia is too tall to hold my hand but too short to walk with arm-in-arm, so we go side-by-side. We cross the railroad tracks and already we're at the Station, with its ripped-out parking lot overlooked by the Shell totem. To our right is the bridge to Wôlinak. I'd like to keep walking in this forgiving light, over and across fields as if this space were finally open and accessible. Instead I speak.

'Here we are. Want to come in and have a drink?'

Antonia isn't sure. My offer doesn't appeal to her. We're both standing here in our day-camp T-shirts: she, barely a young woman; and me, well it's hazy. I could take her in my arms, trace out a dance step on the soft asphalt, thank her for her diligent work.

'It's late. Next time. For the lemonade.'

She gives me a pinched smile, lets go of her backpack strap for an awkward wave goodbye, then turns around. I watch her make her way into the distance, robotic and stiff under my stare, which I know she can feel. I look away, so she can relax.

THE POLICEWOMAN'S STOLEN MIRRORS

She walks out of the gym, makes her way to the drugstore, wants to buy vitamins, in she goes.

The Policewoman walks the aisles, her overheated body flushed red from her workout. She shivers in the air-conditioned coolness. She swivels the sunglass display, wants to try on a pair. There's always some anti-theft device or sticker hanging from the bridge, so you can never be sure they're a good fit. She tries on various pairs and puts them back without checking where they go on the rack. There's a pair with mirrored lenses, *A-ha!* Tries them on, attempts to see her face in the small rectangular mirror that is always placed too high. On tiptoes she turns her head slightly to the right and left. *Not bad. Too much? Nah, let's own it. Badass for real.*

But the anti-theft tag on her nose and the UV rating sticker on the lens is wrecking the effect. She tries to imagine it anyway. Closes her eyes, puckers her lips. But that thing standing in her way is killing her. *How am I supposed to know?* She takes the glasses off for a closer look. First she peels off the sticker, then she checks out the anti-theft tag. Nothing serious: she digs through her side pocket for her switchblade. *Shlack!* She pops the blade and sticks it up against the frame to sever it in a single cut. Kicks aside the low-grade plastic, then folds the knife back up on her thigh and puts it back in her pocket. Her relaxation is palpable. With a comfortable stance, two feet at shoulder width, she places her glasses on her nose and gets back to her charade of checking out different pairs. *Not bad, not bad at all.*

The security guard watches from a distance, seems hesitant. He surveys the scene, looking around for other witnesses. Josée in Cosmetics is demoing a mattifying face cream for an oily-skinned, weary-eyed mother. The other flank is clear. He looks back at the sunglass rack and seems to back up, the woman faces him with only a hint of a smile. He mulls it over but opts for aversion and lets his panoptic glance follow its course over the scene of the crime, then pivots to slowly and deliberately turn his back on this embarrassing scene. He starts walking away with footsteps he wishes were feline yet firm. In truth, he's stiff as a rod. He can feel someone staring at his neck, which makes him warm. He's sweating. Though she has shoplifted a pair of glasses, on his watch, he's the nervous one.

The woman laughs to herself. *That's not everything, I came for something else …* She walks toward the nutritional supplements and grabs a huge jar of protein powder, like a connoisseur. She goes over to pay the cashier with the mirrored sunglasses on the tip of her nose, the better to count out her small change.

The frame zooms in on the mirrored surface of the sunglasses, in which we see the reflection of the policewoman slowly counting coins in her palm.

THE PARADE OF INNOVATION

The air is caustic, the gymnasium full of volunteers and festooned with paper flowers that hang from parallel bars on the walls and dangle from a cable strung across the room. For three days they've been hard at work finishing the floats. First, they built light structures to camouflage the municipal maintenance vehicles: two snowplows on tracks and two pickup trucks. Next they added sheets of Styrofoam. The new vehicles parked outside are still mobile but now blind. Here the swarms of kids from the day camp's captive labour pool have taken over. They've been busy since daybreak pinning the crepe paper flowers they've made to the floats. Outside the gym, three men are nervously making their way across the parking lot with a thematic arch built of loosely conjoined letters for the lead vehicle: *INNOVATION WILL SET US FREE*.

In winter the high-school theatre club was asked to brainstorm a theme for this year's parade. They chose rape culture. 'What the hell kind of theme is that?' asked the principal, dismissing it as impossible to dramatize. 'Well,' answered the club's tall, brazen girls, who had ideas, 'now that you mention it.' But the matter was soon shunted aside, and the theme of industry emerged victorious.

So here we are: floats dedicated to the glory of heavy water, fibre optics, and natural gas. Chimneys spitting out daffodils, a great river shimmering with tiny gold pieces, a storm drain overflowing with hearts, bouquets of cables. The slogan: *Industry & Innovation: Window to the World*. Dream big, they say.

It's parade day.

Mona sits in her truck bed with a beer and a smoke in her mouth, watching the parade. Between the colourful conveyances, costumed students perform a joyful, confused choreography. Mona's waiting to catch a glimpse of her kids. There goes one now. She squints for a better view, to appreciate the costume she threw together. Red tights and shirt, black removable collar, a sheet of flattened green felt worn as a hat – voilà, an only slightly wilted poppy.

Mona's son makes his way uncertainly along, with his entire hand in his mouth, oblivious to the drum guiding them. His hat strap is squeezing his neck a little, she can see. He tries to catch sight of his mother but can't find her. She feels a pang, wants to take him under her wing, pull off everything that scratches him, go for a swim in the river. She takes a swig of beer and whistles sharply. He snaps to attention, his face suddenly and fully present, open, at peace for a moment. Her dirty hand tosses him a kiss. He puts both hands in front of his mouth to blow one back. He wants it to be huge. He watches her receiving it, but already the big walking canola plant behind him is pushing his two hands back into line.

THE AFTERNOON ROLLS BY LIKE A PARADE

The Girl With No Name spent the day with Antonia and the day-camp kids and then slipped off with Mona to skip rocks and drink beer like water by the creek. At one point she fell asleep and woke up achy and insect-bitten in the falling evening. Now she's all alone. Her ears strain to hear the faraway sounds of the festivities at the arena. The music is intercut with an emcee on a one-man mission to get asses out of chairs and shaking. Everybody simply had to *get up on that dancefloor*. She takes in the night, with its smells of dry hay and stagnant water in the abnormally low river.

She gets back on the road. It's almost night, and the hollering is coming nearer. Up ahead in the distance she hears a rowdy group of revellers. She stops and scratches her forearm. The gang springs into action, they're shaking their fists and moving toward her with alarming speed. The Girl With No Name wants to flee, but it's too late. She takes refuge in a phone booth on the sidewalk. Already they're upon her, surrounding her; she sees them first in outline, then up close, wearing muddy overalls, holding big beers. Now they're banging on the phone booth walls. They jump and push and shove, and some press their faces and roll their glassy red eyes against the Plexiglas carved with words both hateful and loving.

She clamps her open hands over her ears to block out their yelling, terrified as a child, and she screams, turning around to force them all to mark her presence. And in a flash, just like they appeared, the gang is gone, as if answering some silent, imperious command. The Girl With No Name remains still for a long time, panting. Her arms are at her sides. Under the desolate light of the disconnected phone booth, she sweats profusely as their screams ring in her ear. There is not, in the empty village, even one soul she can turn to.

No fade to black this time.

The jump cut with no transition signifies
the proximity of danger at the heart of
everyday life.

JULY 4

I make another bowl of cereal. The colour of these chocolate flakes is a false promise, they taste nothing like the unctuous brown on the packaging, which might have warmed me some. Instead I'll have to wait for the milk to take on something of their hue and sickly sweetness. More than the colour, it's the way the flakes grow soggy that comforts me, their texture gentle as a mother's unruffled love.

I eat soft foods in large quantities because I'm afraid. We're all afraid, and this is our solidarity. Or our substance. Or our future. We know there's something we must reject, and with it also something we must want, but we can locate it only within our shared rejection. Our action is false-bottomed, like a trick suitcase.

JULY 6

I'm daydreaming, imagining that we're running.

It's summer and it's hot. The flies are sticking to us, the chickens are clucking, caluckalucking in their nauseating, impenetrable buildings, the wasps are still stinging us though the bees are dying off, and the cattle are lowing, and we're running down the dirt roads. As we go down these never-ending roads, hunger catches up with us. So we snap off spears of wheat, and without stopping to rest our dusty fingers scrape out the kernels that would have become bread. When you chew them long enough it makes a gummy paste. Then the hunger stops gnawing, then this rustic solitude can be enough.

Bare-chested and in baggy pants held up with a length of jute, I'm working. It's hot. The sun is high, sweat runs between my breasts as I chip away at the blacktop with a pick. I stop to take a breath and adjust the scarf that holds back my hair. I pull a big handkerchief from my pocket and wipe off my face, neck, chest, and stomach. Then I get back to work.

I load the chunks I've chipped off into a wheelbarrow that I push and dump in a pile on road's shoulder. I pick up one piece and take a close look, squint to better appreciate its smooth, bluish top and pebbly bottom. It's a wonder to me how, prised free from the illusory cohesion of the surface, the small chunk becomes a world unto itself. Its story begins where its edges tear and fray. Or at least that's where it becomes visible, some substance escaping its foreordained fate. I lay the chunk to rest on the pile with its brethren. *Good luck.*

When I lean over to grab my pick, my breasts jiggle into my field of vision. I'm suddenly half naked. I look around – there's no one. But no matter. With my arms crossed on my chest, I pick up and put on my shirt, which I'd hung on a post. I button it up and tuck the tails into my carpenter's pants, relieved. Sit down on my pile of gravel and pull a cigarette from the pack in my shirt pocket. *Where's my damn lighter?* Here, right-hand pocket. I breathe in deeply, and the smoke goes straight to my head.

How can we both occupy this land and leave the space open? How to slip gently into its networks without upsetting the fragile life we cannot see? Though I want to smash this surface to pieces, I also already regret my action. In springtime we might have lain out on this surface, warmed ourselves with the scarce heat only just starting to build.

Antonia knows the highways well. She learned from her father, Peter, when they'd hitchhike. They didn't have a car, and he refused to take the bus. *What bus am I gonna take around here, anyway?* he'd say. *You see a bus anywhere?*

They grappled up on-ramps, daughter guiding father, scowling in the disheartening cold. He feared nothing, not even being swallowed up in the mechanical swarm of vehicles. A car would always stop, eventually, or sometimes a truck intrigued by this fragile duo of young girl and tall skinny man. When they realized he was blind, a heavy silence clouded over their good deed: what kind of careless goddamn lunatic goes out in this cold and *with a child, to boot.* She'd grown used to their commiseration. His father ignored it, turning his extinguished gaze outward onto the unfolding landscape. She imagined that one day she'd just leave him there. A car would stop and no one would see the driver's outstretched arm flipping the lock, opening the door, reaching out a hand. And Antonia would seize her chance, get in the car, and slam shut the door in her father's face.

She can almost hear the squealing brakes as the driver peels out and speeds off, without waiting for more. She sees herself turning toward the man at the steering wheel and giving him a broad grin, mouth half-open over her small, childish, insouciant teeth. He would look at her with an uncertain smile, barely a glance in the rear-view to scope the blind man's reaction. And if he looked again he'd lose sight of the father, disappearing from view over the crest of the hill. And he'd be right to worry. Because she never takes her eyes off his mouth and his eyes and his hair blowing in the wind and his dimples, so he tosses his butt out the window and grips the wheel with both hands, his arms straining with hope and desire for her.

Antonia hears the sacred music of the spheres. I know she's there, know without seeing her, because of the music that follows her wherever she goes and that holds my world together through its vital necessity. I dread the day when she will wake up and her movement will take her far away somewhere, and I'll no longer hear anything at all.

Blurrily, through a frame constructed of two hands, in an imitation of binoculars, a highway carries Antonia away.

JULY 14

The junked car's axles are up on logs, its hood ripped off, its useful parts stripped. But the four doors close well enough to give us a shelter of sorts. If we have no choice but to hide our love away from the Station and your mother's stares, this is the place. When I clamber out after fucking, the moss is warm on my feet; it's summer. And when I climb in to sit on you, with my back to your face, I see your eyes in the rear-view, your eyes that go white before composure returns and your mouth that bites my neck and your hand reaching up to my damp breasts and your thumb pressing on my pulsing neck vein. When the moon is high, I can see our reflection in the windshield, four hands on my breasts and my stomach and the sight of this, our little drive-in movie, makes me cum.

You're grooving to the music, smoking like a cowboy with arms like propellers on his hunched shoulders, the world perfectly fitted to your body, oh you know you can dance to anything. We brush up against each other with beer foam on our upper lips and rub our noses in each other's hair. All we need is a boom box up on the car roof. It's enough for a party, a party of two.

This morning they're swinging picks, tearing up the worn-out blacktop.

Gaby's making regular trips to Montreal. This time he brought Mathieu and his brother, who plan to stay awhile. And Claire is here too, back for a week with her girlfriend and their capricious bitch of a dog. Attempts to train her fail so miserably that we dub her 'Catastrophe.'

Claire has schemes to enrich our compost, remediate the soil. There's nitrogen, carbon, urine … The Girl With No Name is preoccupied with other things, but she pees where they tell her to. She likes the feeling of her naked ass out in the fresh air.

At this moment she's making her way over the broken ground, lifting her eyes toward the yellow shell on its perch, as she turns in a circle with her hands on her hips. The shed has been cleared of old tires and junk. Two small rooms on the ground floor have been set up as laboratory and darkroom; a shiny woodstove that Mona found somewhere sits in the middle of the main room. A ladder leads up to the large attic. Mattresses have been laid out carefully and evenly, beds freshly made; it's welcoming. *Welcoming for whom?* she wonders.

She sits out on the porch with a creased forehead, beside the Old Man, who is puzzling over a Sudoku.

Without looking up, he asks, 'What's bothering you?'

She sighs. 'We can't keep going like this.'

'What do you mean, *like this?*'

'Self-sufficient. Closed off to the world.'

'We're not that closed off. I got in.'

'Well, technically *we* moved into *your* place.'

He cocks an eye in her direction and runs a lustful tongue over his lips.

'Works for me.'

She doesn't get up. Her gaze is inward, focused.

'I can see why they're not friendly. We just kind of showed up and act like we own the place.'

She thinks back to the episode in the phone booth, still surprised that she so feared the carnival.

'I mean, this place don't belong to them,' says the Old Man. 'The dirt-roaders. No more than it's ours. Folks out in Wôlinak, that's another story … *We're* in *their* home.'

She gets up. 'Still, we should do something, I guess. Introduce ourselves at least. Have them over for a cookout.'

The Old Man looks up, vaguely exasperated. But she's not done.

'We could build a spit. You must know how to do that, right?'

That very night at the weekly gathering around the totem shell, the Girl With No Name puts forward her idea. Mona has taken Gaby on her knee, like a shy tame fox. She caresses the top of his head, protests that such a feast would be pearls for this local swine.

The Girl With No Name ignores her. In the end, the group approves, a date is set, tasks assigned. People are into it, why not? They still have to find an animal and figure out how to kill and prepare it. They watch the Old Man squirming in his chair.

'Hold on a minute. I never killed a hog. Heard they squeal like babies.'

The Girl With No Name looks up to the heavens and sighs sharply.

'Not a hog, a lamb. The animal to roast on a spit is a lamb.'

People keep talking, adjusting their plans, casting around for ideas. The Old Man bites his nails in silence, brow furrowed, annoyed.

The next days go by in preparations for the feast. Mona picks fresh herbs to dress the animal. People beg and borrow dishes and cutlery. Claire and the Girl With No Name go out for drinks and ice.

One evening the lamb shows up in the back of Mona's pickup. We pull it down with all the care one would lavish on an eminent guest and put it on a long leash in the yard, at the edge of a field where it can graze. Mona's kids play with it, like a stuffed animal. Claire keeps her mad dog close. Our lamb will be slaughtered on Feast Day, here on this small pedestal.

FEAST DAY

The lamb has been bled out. It didn't go as planned, under a butcher's expert hands. Instead its neck was torn open by the jaws of Catastrophe the dog.

After a moment of chaos amid human yells and the yapping of the offending bitch, the Old Man took things in hand. The others work alongside him, helping gut and skin the beast.

The townsfolk showed up in small groups, too early. They're on their best behaviour, have traded twelve-packs for fancier bottles, brought nachos and dip. *Just put that down wherever.* There are small families and couples and young boys in little groups. The hosts from the Station are filthy, their hands are bloody, the sound system won't work. It's tense. The Girl With No Name hides out for a minute in the outhouse, head in hands, gathering flies. *Stupid stupid stupid plan!*

But eventually the moment comes into its own and everyone relaxes. The fire crackles, the lamb turns on its spit, the day draws out. A small crew from Wôlinak has gathered round the fire. To mend the rift caused by the dog and soften up the deeper ones still tearing at our skins, people start singing songs. The sound system kicks in.

Antonia's here with her father. Catastrophe sits by the blind potter's side. He keeps the animal from getting into trouble, his hand like a magnet for Catastrophe to slobber over. Antonia doesn't eat a bite: she nervously watches people going about their business and takes a drink now and then, bent over the fire and listening to the singing, before finally falling asleep with her head on the knees of the Girl With No Name, who is in a sort of trance. Another woman was there, but she went unseen. She took a tour around the fire, solitary and distant behind her mirrored sunglasses, barely nodding hello to the people she knows, and refusing any hint of familiarity.

By morning the whole field is trampled flat and they have found a peace of sorts. Everyone sleeps late, in deep woodsmoke-scented repose.

OUR STORY PEELS OUT IN A RED CORVETTE

Canella's red Corvette skids to a halt under the totem. She slithers out. From the passenger door a large body extends a limb. Her baaabe. The Girl With No Name is on the porch.

The hefty bruh is back with his baby-doll. Already his hand is scooping her ass, pushing it toward her.

(The Girl With No Name takes the baton.)

I'm going down, diving deep. Nothing will happen outside this fantasized space.

They come closer, not much distance between us now I go downstairs we walk toward each other. I pull him forward for a kiss, the guy whose hands are playing patty-cake with her plastic Barbie ass. We form a walking daisy chain, interlaced, I manage to catch her mouth I grab his cock we're actors in the wings waiting for our second act. This same totem that towers over us in darkness shall light our way again. I bite her lips she takes off my shirt my breasts come free their hands on my incorrigible fleshy body, I feel their hunters' prowess swelling behind me, straining against my ass through the fabric of my underwear, his cock pressing up on me sturdy enough to carry me off and she's sucking on my tits they're growing hard I tug down her shorts her ass and pussy are exposed to the air now my fingers work her clear-cut waxed-smooth mound as I spread her slit and open wide her scrunched-up lips emit a little squelch like forest moss, so out of keeping with her skin so soft she's slick I lick her open mouth he squeezes me against her she pulls down his shorts from behind my panties too I'm naked unprotected from his hard dick seeking a passage I turn to him suck on his lips and she's behind me now, T-shirt cast off and silicone breasts pressing against my shoulder blades he tongues my groove then thrusts his cock into my hairy cunt. We climb into the back of Mona's pickup truck I lie down on top of the big dude and his dick slides right inside me while Canella eats my ass and I imagine her poor tight ass up in the air with no one to tend to it I pull out his cock push her down on all fours and take the swollen hot dick in my mouth then let it go to lick her hole and then I suck on it some more, that impatient dick that wants back inside me so bad, I run my tongue up and down, slowly, languorously up and down each interlocking piece so keen to fit together and when I step aside he pulls her glistening plastic ass toward him and embeds himself inside she arches her back she resists I roll under her to suck her breasts her mouth I'm eating and with her attention elsewhere she offers up her ass he stuffs it full again and again and again and then takes out his cock it slips I put it back inside her snatch she coos with pleasure and I want him it's my turn now and under her I spread my dripping lips and pull his long hard shaft away from her wet clatch and into me instead, and now he's on top of me, smiling. I hold his dick and oh-so-gently brush its tip with my lips, I'm smiling too. Time is suspended his look is fraught everything is a question of momentum and tension. Then he assumes the position again runs his tongue over my mouth and bites it again and shoves it in again and again this fucking never fucking ends it never ends he moves so far to give me a shine-coat of sweat, he's so engorged I want to do what he's doing too, force open his ass, or else watch someone do it for me. Canella's clinging to him from behind, straddling him rubbing her juicy hairless pussy over his back which is way too wide for her, she is twiddling her twig and I know the sullen teen-ager is out on the porch, watching us, I can tell he's taken off headphones and I want him to come over, throw his hat in the ring. He's there and he's watching Canella rub herself spread-eagle he gets up on the platform he takes out his dick and starts jerking it off to the show too young to even know where to put it with so many gleaming possibilities wide open and welcoming the big guy has flipped me over my ass is tight between his hands his dick is grinding but Canella pushes him away and pulls it out of me, she wants some too. The sullen teen's hair is down over his face and now he's slowly taking off his clothes letting loose he's muscular like a mechanic's apprentice his stance is firm his tool outstretched and flapping in the wind, unsupported. He cranes his neck to check out our bodies I catch his eye from every direction draw him toward me so he can put it in me so his glans rubs against the other big guy's I want them to cry out from the pain of being unable to endure another moment of being handled. I grab the young cat's tail and rub it over my stomach and mouth, it slips over my breasts he sucks them voraciously, still desperately seeking mommy but I have other plans for you my friend you're going to drink your daddy's milk come over big guy come over and rub your dick on his ass he's irresistible c'mon give it a try it's your turn take a shot rock that pole the tiger has turned around they're both bent over toward each other rubbing off dick to dick coffee-coloured with a shiny cherry centre purplish fleshy they grab each other's shoulders to go down down down on our wide-open mouths and suck at our tongues our hot cunts are dripping all over enfolding each other we're lapping away to warm them up, and whose ass will open up first to who, let's make a bet.

AUGUST 9

Mona's truck is in front of the Station again this morning. I go out on the porch. The Old Man is coming back in from the woods. He stops and scowls in front of the burnt-out totem. As his hunterly forces wane, he must go deeper and deeper into the thinning woods to replenish them. He walks by the pickup truck. Slaps the hood, gives me a look. I leave the porch and go to the kitchen; he comes too. A strong smell clings to cheeks white from the beard overgrowing them. I love nothing more than when he comes back, his body recharged and blind. Ever so gently I sidle up, ease off my shirt. He lays his brown hands on my white breasts. We stay there, iron to magnet, his warm palms massaging my tits, his hands small cages containing them. We stay that way until the honking horn from Mona's truck pulls us apart. I get in.

Mona wants to show me a spot, an unearthed stone covered in psychotropic lichen. On the dead rock there is a living substance that Mona brews into infusions that shuffle our egos and then deal out the pieces in a new order, like cards from a deck. Sex brings me to the edge of exhaustion, but not outside myself like this. As orgasm fades I fall back to the point of gravity; my curtailed momentum pins me to the ground when all I want is to be lifted up.

Mona makes her way through a field of grass up to her shoulders. She turns around to see where I am. I stop to listen to the buzzing of insects dislodged by her passage, a warm summer sound that envelops us. Her wiry body wends a path through the nettles and arrow-leaved smartweed and cow parsnip.

'Watch you don't get a rash,' she yells out over her pointed shoulder. And she's off, *frrr frrr*.

Suddenly all goes quiet. We've reached the edge of a forest, where the tall grasses stop growing and where they will wait for our return. We have to get down on all fours and crawl through the branches, find purchase on mossy rocks and twisted roots. Mona is the Spirit of the Forest and all I have to do is follow in her footsteps, as if nature has recognized a kindred spirit and cleared a path for one more of its forms. I don't take my eyes off her, my focus runs along the furrow she has ploughed for me, a bridge for me to cross.

Lots of light now. Mona is hewing a clearing. In the middle stands a massive rock, so wide it calls to mind something man-made, a cardboard menhir.

I laugh hard and then black out from the lichen dropped under my tongue. I'm tripping, and I have a vision.

I see Antonia at the foot of a tree, she wants to climb. Something vague holds her back: a force or its opposite, an impotence. She examines the trunk, foresees every foothold, has every step to the top figured out. But her body stays stiff as a log, glued to the moist earth. She wants a head start. Her immobility is gathered time and she doesn't know whether it's lost or stored to fuel her motion, catapult her forward.

From where I stand, I want to urge her on. *You're strong, come on!*

Her father watches her, unseeing, from the porch. She lowers her head. Behind his pressed-shut eyelids and this false resignation, some mysterious substance is being distilled and carbureted, fuel for interstellar flight. Antonia grew up at the heart of a commune, passed from arm to arm, learning and experimenting and building new worlds. Now she inhabits a deserted fiefdom, barren of illusions. She is gathering and gathering and gathering the strength to pop open the bottle.

I have a vision of Antonia and me. I say, out loud, 'We're walking side-by-side, arm-in-arm,' as if I've unearthed some magnificent truth. *Antonia, my Antonia.* Our twin shadows project our age difference onto an indifferent flat surface. Antonia refuses to play. I admire her tense inertia. Side by side we walk through the prickly grasses, whistling. From afar I say hello to her father, who sits there like a forgotten toy. Only his daughter's presence now sparks him to life. From time to time I see an old woman. She walks with a limp but is sharp as a tack, shaking a fist at us without stepping down from the porch. She stays safe on her high ground, with Antonia her one link to the outside world. The garden, the mailbox, the road. Antonia is free to go where she pleases.

Her features blur. Antonia vanishes.

Now it's the group from the Station I see.

Their bodies are visionary, hallucinatory. They are entranced. Images of the Hauka appear from a Jean Rouch film, *Les maîtres fous*: eyes rolling back in their sockets, distended veins forming knots on the surfaces of sweaty skin. At the Station they are twisting what they've learned in university, plugging their experiences into alternate circuits, tucking away the chips of insight that don't fit on any shelf. They sing songs as they write out the lines of an invented code. They are fighting the System, they are ruffling feathers, throwing spanners into works. They're actors on this world stage, a full cast of characters and systems – judge, lawyer, kernel and dependencies, geeks and silicone yuppies with air-conditioned buses, five-star cafeterias, cloistered executives. There is the driving force of change, and a manifesto to put words to it. I see them dancing at the foot of the burnt-out totem at our abandoned gas station, drunk like survivors, their bodies whirling backward. This dance will take me back to them. I yell out spells, flashes of heat that burn their hands. They have a thousand arms with which they toss me up, far beyond whatever it is we normally protect ourselves against.

I come down, somehow.

Now we're driving in the dark. The hot truck clunks along reassuringly. Mona lets go of the wheel a minute to stroke my head.

Then we're back at the Station. Everyone is there, even the sullen teen, though he sticks to his phone, giving us the side-eye. A serious discussion is underway. They're counting rooms. What's the bare minimum to build an accelerator? There's nothing we need that we can't figure out how to make ourselves. The work progresses faster than our understanding of it. They've slept so little that their eyes are scarcely open.

We pull up two chairs. The Old Man boils water, gets out the booze. There are a lot of us: a new girl and three guys have joined our ranks and are planning to stay for a while, till October when they have to go back to Italy. I like the woman's name, *Frainetti*, and its associations: Arletty, frenesy, spaghetti, friend of me.

SUBJECT IDENTIFICATION

Last name: FRAINETTI
First name: Ida
Date of birth: 11.09.1987
Place of birth: MONTREAL
Country of birth: CANADA
Country of citizenship: CANADA
Sex: FEMALE
Mother's names (first and last):
Gabrielle HOULE
Father's names (first and last): Luigi
FRAINETTI
Address: Via Pietro Calvi 29 20 129,
Milan, ITALY

Roving surveillance underway since November 3, 2008, by the Criminal Intelligence Service of Québec, in the vicinity of the building at ███████████ (former SHELL station) in the municipality of ██████████ has led to the following determinations:

1. Transport of unidentified individuals.

At the time appearing at the head of this document dated August 9, 2009, we observed:

The individual identified as Ida FRAINETTI
being transported along the roadway toward the residence of ████████████████████

Facts recorded in the file:
Individual Ida FRAINETTI arrived on Cana-
dian soil on May 10, 2009, from Milan,
Italy.

JOURNAL OF THE GIRL WITH NO NAME

SEPTEMBER 3

We get regular visitors from France and Ireland and the United States. The Italians are different, though. Friends of friends, mostly, intrigued by the Station. They come to be inspired, or just lend a hand and enjoy the trip for a while. Some show up out of nowhere and leave without a trace; others let us know they're coming; they post selfies in front of the accelerator we're building. They bunk in the shed or camp in the back fields. Resource-rich: none come empty-handed. We're a link in a circular economy. Cars arrive with full trunks and leave behind guidebooks and materials to set up the Station.

We have no manifestos, just 'open' anarchist spaces that are horizontally organized with pernicious hierarchies and often little to set them apart from start-ups. They share the same entrepreneurial zeal, don't bother denying it. People learning by doing, making it up as they go along, thirsty for knowledge like students who have slipped the bonds of desiccated institutions. Some will get rich for sure, find applications for their research. Not for a moment do they doubt that they will *make the world a better place*, but that alone is not enough to give their work direction. They ask for nothing, promise nothing. *We have no program; we are the program.* We move forward as if parting the sea, opening a precarious groove in which to make something, and we won't know what until we're done. The Law continues its inexorable forward march, measuring and surveying and leaving a succession of closed spaces in its wake. I'm there too, following along, but The Law is ever nipping at our heels.

I love how power is concentrated but porous at the edges. How I can pass through at will. In this middle of nowhere, where no one believes in us and no plot can frame us, we make things by hand, we make things in plain sight.

I don't know how to do anything. Don't know how to produce anything. But I keep going, will keep going until I'm pushed over the edge by the problem I'm working on: to see whether some other kind of sex exists that I will only find by doing. I am our field unit's Department of Intuition. My research concentration is the flesh. My personal revolution is based on principles I copy from the others. Before the natural laws of love, I too run. I attach myself to one and all, like a burr stuck in a sweater, pulling at threads, opening up a hole. It's a lot of work: not to seek to possess, to accept false promises, to be ghosted and ignored like so many other positions and figures. Because everything's a matter of position. In bed with my ass up and out in the open air, or on my back with my stomach arched up, or crouching on all fours, my life is open wide; I try out all manner of positions, from the ones that are a strain to those I fall easily into. Out of bed it is more of the same. I get attached to other people's movements and actions, like so many railings I can walk along. So long as I build up sufficient momentum and they are strong enough to bear my weight, I won't fall.

I'm spending more and more time in the woods. I learn about plants at Mona's side and the Old Man teaches me about snares, while I wait for Antonia at the school gate or for my next tryst at the junked car. Frainetti has also enlisted me. We meander through the county, exploring its hidden corners.

Am I really trustworthy? I wonder. Consistently trust-worthy – *Can I really be trusted?*

If I were a table I'd have legs planted firmly on the ground and an even level top. I'd be stable and solid, so solid that no one would question me as they put down their groceries or their papers to work, their dishes or their elbows to sit down. Not once would anyone stop to wonder whether I could bear the weight. If I were a table, or a mother.

MEMORY OF AN INTERROGATION

The man is suburban avuncular. Overly tanned for the time of year, he wears a khaki suit with a striped tie: red, white, blue, red, white, blue, and so on and so forth such that you cannot tell which came first, red or white or blue. The windowless room with low-hanging fluorescents seems at odds with his necktied bonhomie.

The boy and girl in front of him don't know why they've been summoned. Behind their determined air there runs a tension: should they refuse point blank or play the game, sing for their suppers. Two of them and the man makes three, but they hail from irreconcilable worlds.

The man with the striped tie is laying it on thick. Every move he makes is cut from the cheap cloth of mass-market cop shows, from his shiny shirt straining more tightly at his gut than at his pecs to his sleeves rolled up to denote a 'man of action,' the way his pants hug his hips, the chunky dad-watch at his wrist, and the bulge of his crotch. His sizeable package stiffens as he stares at the girl. Her breasts roam free under her T-shirt, taunting him: *Look here, it's everything that you will never have.* Mr. Necktie overplays his hand like a ham actor. He tries to sit down on the corner of his desk, the better to lean over them, but the movement brings forth a little fart. His face loses countenance while surprise and a hint of a laugh ripple the others', subverting the balance of power. They are the audience of two to this man's performance, and it's not going well. Sweat is pearling under the foundation, the pores in his skin that he tries to conceal are earthy craters compromising the image of power he so wants to project. Their foreign, mocking looks counteract the man's charm, so rarely cast in doubt here; their look breaches his defences, infiltrates and multiplies.

He, a known quantity in this room, familiar to the walls and furniture against and on which he has groped his interns, did not in any way expect this, especially on home turf. Nor was he prepared for the violent uncontainable desire he now feels for them both. In the light of their scorn he's overheating. He wants to grab the girl's head and pull it up against his throbbing crotch, let her feel up close who's in charge here, so that later, when he lets her go, she'll replay the scene in her head, reach down and rub one out while she imagines him taking her. The police fantasies have taken root in the rich soil of his projections, which lash out in every direction – don't even get him started on the ethnics and crazy women, sluts and welfare bums and art fags … you've heard it before.

But these two are different, somehow. They're not afraid, and that stokes his desire. It's personal, somehow. Something between her and him, them and him, their parts and his. When he looks over at the boy, a violent desire seizes him, he feels his asshole opening. The slender nape of that neck, the insolent brown clumps of hair dancing between his collar and his smooth skin, his legs so nonchalantly spread. *I'm gonna unbutton your jeans and pull them down around your ankles, along with your underwear. I'll push you up against the wall. Thrust my nightstick into your tight muscular anus, and then grab your rod and you'll push it into my wide-open, lubed-up ass, and the girl will join us, lick us up and down while her pussy swells and we'll take each other, one another, one against the other sucking each other's dicks whenever we pull them from her juicy cunt, and now our twin tongues in her anus, eating her open hole in an infinite embrace.*

He wants them both. He wants to give them everything, tell them everything. He wants to be loved, and in humiliating supplication he murmurs, *Take me with you, don't leave me alone.*

SEPTEMBER 10

I'm running behind Frainetti and my hair is in my eyes and those eyes never leave the feet running frantically ahead of me. *Wait for me, you're going too fast*, I say, over and over again like a mantra, even my thoughts are panting. We're already at the chain-link fence, we'll have to hop it. She stops just long enough to find footholds, then starts climbing. *Hurry up!* she says, raising her arms and lifting her legs over to the other side. I'm next: a foot here, one there, and hands up higher; then my foot slips and my full body weight is resting on my fingertips. I catch myself and pull myself back up to the top, where I extend my leg and pull it over, trembling. I'm stuck here now, trying to maintain balance while I lift my left leg over the top of the fence. She's down below me on the other side, arms stretched out toward me, *C'mon, jump, bend your legs*. I hear the guards behind me, getting closer. *Back up!* I yell. Then I jump.

Time feels unnaturally prolonged, like falling off a bike. But no amount of time spent staring at the ground will cushion your fall.

I fall again, feet and hands on the ground. I have to get back up, push forward on the broken springs of my legs.

But then I'm running again. Faster this time. The chain-link fence protects our escape. My fear no longer slows my momentum.

We run for a long a while on Leblanc Road, and it's dark; if it weren't for the moon we wouldn't be able to see the chewed-up blacktop, a metallic grey strip between fields of soybeans already dry in their pods. The road is straight, the earth is flat, there's no one chasing us now.

As we run, our heavy breathing tries to settle into a rhythm. To our right we pass Missouri Road, which we know leads to Precieux-Sang where Mona lives, although we've never been there. We come to the Wôlinak gate, have to pass through to get back on the way to the river, the bridge, and the Station. Silent silhouettes of animal statues stand in front of the small white church – one, two, three, four, all reassuring presences, none of which will pounce on us.

We run to get away. We run to breathe. We run like animals, our senses finely honed, proud to find this strength inside ourselves. We could run all night under a moon like this.

Back at the Station, I rip off my bag, unbutton my jacket, throw it on a hook, and collapse onto the red couch. Frainetti stays outside, smoking on the porch. The Old Man's there too, slouched over a Sudoku puzzle.

'Got a light?' he asks, with a smoke already in his mouth.

'No, but I'm thirsty.'

'One day you'll get caught. I don't want to be there when it happens.'

'You won't. That's one thing I know for sure.'

'They'll beat your ass. Leave you out in the woods. And you'll lie there until some guy or his dog go out to piss against a tree, or some Indian finds you out there.'

'You'll find me. You know the woods.'

He brought someone else to our tryst at the junked car. It shattered something inside me. I was a surfer riding a wave through the ruins of Pacific Ocean Park, and it was all good, and then a concrete column appeared. When I slammed into it, my confidence unhitched.

He's there, sitting on the dented roof. He's there but not alone: I see another back beside his. I clench up, my hands grow clammy, my stomach knots up, and not out of desire. My mind races. I try to understand the reason for this kink in our plan, pretend I'm not gutted. They can't see me yet. I'm behind them, hidden from view by the shrubs that line the path. My fear is telling me something my mind and body already know. I'm neutralized by fear. He slides off the roof and walks over to make his way around the car, but stops, blocking me out with his back, that back that makes my terror swell. Son of a trapper, he's picked up my scent. He can identify the smell of my secretions and saliva. All he wants is to lick. He recognizes the toxins of fear too. The sight of the unseeing back of his neck covered by the hair I've so often grabbed and pulled does something to me ... I try to find words that will oppose this affront. Because that's what he does, by showing tails not heads, not eyes. I am unfaced.

Time stretches out, then I step forward. My old skin has sloughed, I've decided no fate can be as bad as our fears. I step forward and that's my one hope. I step forward toward his ass and muscular back. I move toward his warm hands, toward his dick, I advance despite this other man beside him, who turns around and who I don't know and who lowers his eyes and now jumps off the roof as well.

I go around the car, I want his face, I try to find his eyes. He turns his head and I'm amazed at what I see: not the face of a monster, no drugged-out eyes. His face tells me no more than the back of his neck. It tells me nothing. He reaches out a hand. I dry mine, which are moist, on the edge of my skirt, and I mark in my mind this brief moment when I had the time to wipe hands that were clammy from fear and put them in the hands of the one who will rape me. He pulls me toward him and whispers his plan in my ear. *My friend wants to meet you. Ever since he's been watching us. He knows what to do. How to get you wet, just like me.* The other guy moves forward, to present evidence. I try to look at him, record his features, but nothing comes, his code has been wiped clean, I can't rewrite it. He is devoid of colour and texture. He has no age. There's his cock, which I see when I lower my eyes and he opens his fly to take it out. It's already hard. A cock. And I bring my hand to my mouth to wet the fingers that I hold out to grab it, and I pull back my hand and again bring it to my mouth, to kiss it this time, to kiss it goodbye.

One night under the full moon they play a show. There are three who play guitar, with spoons strung to their sleeves for campfire percussion. They're sitting outside, at the foot of the totem. Together but not in unison they sing, a random collection of songs. They aren't ironic and they don't hold back; they're really giving it their all. They sing off-key, they sing with their whole hearts and mouths wide open. Sometimes conviction flags, and then one of them stretches their limbs, like a cat, lost in a thought, and the others too lose their buzz a bit. But then they swell up together, look it's swelling up again, the music like a wave sweeping us away. Frainetti rides the wave, singing Italian work songs of labour and sunshine.

Mona watches them intently, buzzing around with childlike, full-frontal curiosity. I watch her; I watch them. Frainetti sings loudly, then breaks off into a laugh so full of joy it overflows onto the ground. We are all here, our full forces assembled.

Mona spins around and drinks and I watch Mona. She neither likes nor doesn't like what she sees here, is neither mocking nor approving of this scene. She's ecstatic. She laughs and I walk in her laughter which catches up with me, a link in the chain that binds us more securely than I had at first thought. Mona does not look at me; she doesn't have to, she knows me well enough, she knows me all too well, she knows full well who and where I am. When I see that this is so my heart leaps up, although it also cuts me down to size: *her certainty, her toughness, I love her so bad she'll eat me alive.*

Around the bonfire we gallop like horses. Antonia watches us, timing our laps. I'd love to catch her on our way around but that might only compound her resistance. Antonia doesn't respond to the movement all around her by joining in: she records it and stands still, looking to find another path, sometimes even straying further out. There! She's moving away. She fades from view, outside the totem's halo, and I seek her out with my eyes, but I'm running too fast, I can't see. I think I see the trapper laying a hand on her shoulder, but already I'm turning my back to them and the others are passing between them and me. They're running too. Our bonfire is alive. On my next go round I don't see her at all. The Old Man's there in her place, but she's gone. A hairline crack of fear has fissured my joy that was just now so certain. The long-dry well of fossil-fuel geysers is soaking the ground, dousing all that burned bright just a moment ago in a cooling, leaden heaviness. Mona's a psychotic alcoholic, a Vardian vagabond who will never again love another soul. To whose wagon have I hitched my own? My heart clenches tight. I'm every bad mother who ever lived.

I'm walking along with a big pointed papier mâché hat on my head and a mask of dry clay that won't let me talk or even smile. When I make a face it sends little clots raining down over my big white cape. It's uncomfortable, itchy.

I sit on a stump in the middle of a field to think about this story I'm writing. I'm worried about the girl who disappeared. My Antonia. Her disappearance feels like the start of something, but what? Will it upset the balance for those of us left? Will we send out a search party? I'm afraid the world as we know it will crumble without her, leaving a scattering of aimless people grasping at the straws of a bygone era. I try to reassure myself. *What of it? Is not a crumbling still a movement? She's the one that matters here. What she's looking for matters more than any expedition we could send out after her.*

No one ever knows whether they'll reach their destination, nor what will open up for them there. There is only one true future, the one we walk toward with bent backs.

Antonia treads in the footsteps of others. Some were free, yet mothers still, doing their best to care for the children who cross their paths and young women assailed with doubt. They struggle to create some value that might circulate freely, under no orders; some value that might support all girls, the ones they have been and the ones they still are and all the others who might be in need.

They have *thoughts* about how things go badly, and yet there's love still and you have to want to give it, still, against all odds, in the middle of this battlefield.

SEPTEMBER 20

Another one shows up, uninvited. Not Mona, not Frainetti: a policewoman. She's simply there one morning when I come downstairs. She's just there in her uniform, the blue of authority. I look up at her face, she does not smile. I'm in my pyjamas, yawning and soft all over, in stark contrast with her body, which is harnessed to her work and the established order. I can feel my breasts moving around in my tank top, and I have no idea how to hide myself away. But I enjoy the messiness of it.

The Old Man is there too, refilling her coffee. He points to the coffee pot; I nod; he pours me some into a glass he sets down on the table. All these details come rushing at me, exerting pressure on my corneas and my memory. I'm making an archive, straining to support my newfound acuity, recording every detail while keeping an eye on the policewoman. The density of a given substance is manifest in a million signs, and it's my job to watch for them. Time slows to let this stream of consciousness flow through me. I feel myself fully present. I am not on edge, I'm fully open. My thoughts still have room for my breasts, which are liable to pop out every time I lean over. I see her looking, aware of that risk; I see her blinking eyes and sense her sizing me up: ingénue or agent provocateur? She holds her cup more tightly, though it's too hot in the morning air. She holds her cup like it's the only way to keep her hand from working its way down the shaft of her nightstick, which crept up her hips when she sat down.

I recognize her as the woman I saw at the gym with Antonia.

The nightstick has crept over the horizon of the table, the hint of a threat that never quite leaves and you never get used to. I'm stretching. I want her to see my breasts pop out, want to watch her grow hot under her polyester collar, hot in her vest and those god-awful pants and those butt-ugly shoes. I want her to feel the useless, punitive weight of the accessories of her position. Ultimately I want her rage to mirror my own. She looks away from my soft arms and undulating breasts and my stomach offered up on display and my belly button, a hole some people like to lick, but that she only threatens.

The Old Man's arms are crossed. He doesn't like what he sees, I know. He doesn't like it when we are not all on equal footing. I don't care. Let him be pissed. I'll do what I want and right now what I want is to strut like a peacock. My freedom is expanding, swelling up at the sight of the sweaty awkwardness of a policewoman too encumbered and heavily armed for the calm of our kitchen. Haloes of damp are forming under her arms that she has difficulty crossing because of her many straps. There are straps on her shirt, straps for her nightstick. But this is the life she chose. What would make a person want to spy, investigate, beat other people's bodies? I look over her face and I see what it is: she wants to play.

She's staring at my breasts, not looking me in the eye, though she can feel mine on her. Now she's the one looking me up and down. She leans her head over too, weighing the evidence gathered by her look. With her right hand she fingers her nightstick and oh-so-gently unsheathes it. Before it's out, I am struck. *But that's a sword!* I think, *How ridiculous, this cop thinks she's a Jedi knight,* but then she reaches the tip of the baton and sets it down to rest between us. It's thick more than long and made of something unreflective and unthinking, black, matte. She points it at me and half stands up to lean over the table and the coffee cups and the sugar box and the full array of everyday objects that suggest we are not criminals – the butter knife sprawled out on the dish, the crumbs and coffee rings on the oilskin cloth. She half stands up and reaches out, holding her nightstick, which she brushes against my breast. It's not a blow, it's a caress.

Her face pinches with effort as she circles my breast. She's playing, taking pleasure, and she has regained the power. This power doesn't grow out of her nightstick, it resides in her willingness to push the game further.

(*The policewoman isn't stupid.*)

You thought (she thinks), Here I am, almost naked, free and light my ass soft in my panties tits rubbing on the thin fabric of my camisole, firming up in the certitude that everyone is excited by them, and now here you are looking at me, power-less … *That's what you thought* (she thinks). *Look at you now surrounded by all these unyielding materials … You've brought this disorder upon yourself, you didn't believe I'd play this game with you, you never thought I'd use my police gear for play and my power to force open your desire.*

Power abides, enseams the earth with radioactive wastes that catch fire often and sometimes forever. Human power is a living, circulating substance; reactive and treacherous, it holds us and fills us up and distributes its spoils – it's her or it's me, her again or both of us or me, and neither one of us can believe what's happening or who has washed up like flotsam.

If I back down she wins and then she's free to shove her stick wherever she wants. I want to melt down her nightstick until it's just raw lead, not this quivering cock I want to feel up inside me. As gently as she leaned over the table, I plant my feet and arch my back. I take off my camisole and free my breasts, which are buzzing from my morning coffee and warming my veins in the already cool Bécancour morning. She hasn't moved, but I see sweat pearling on the peach fuzz above her upper lip. Her grip on the stick must be slippery in her moist palms. She tightens it up, leans over a touch further, grabs onto the edge of the table to shift her weight toward me. I feel the nightstick, a stronger pressure now. Shifting from one breast to the other, she traces the outline of my nipples, slides down to my belly button and eases her stick under the elastic waistband of my panties, then tries to push further down. *I'll give her a hand*, I think, *I'll take them off.*

The Old Man is rubbing his face, both hands, I know he's hard, but he hasn't drunk enough to let loose in the harsh lighting of this theatre. He glances over, rubs his face. It's more than he can handle. I feel sorry for him and hold back, though I want to rip off my clothes. The policewoman also puts her investigation on hold. She's known him since childhood. As her body matured, he was watching from afar. He sized her up, like the animals he catches in his snares. He has seen her working out to build her muscles for combat, to provoke him. Her desire to push forward, driven by strength and fear, is what made her a sexual being in his eyes. He has whacked off to the memory of the time she caught him driving without a licence. She saw him staring at her breasts, hands on his shorts, a hard lump under the steering wheel, her breasts straining her shirt after she handed over the ticket, her chest thrusting toward him when he got out of the car, in breach of the law.

He did not fear her. He beat off in his car with his head cocked back, imagined her breasts swinging freely from her open shirt as she rode him.

Not like this, though. No, that would be going too far. He grabs the nightstick, which the policewoman resheathes without complaint, and picks up my camisole and puts my head through the opening, and I slide one arm in, and then the other. *You've got nothing to lose by waiting.* She sits back down and I do too.

'She came about the girl,' he says.

Antonia has disappeared.

IS SHE TOO YOUNG TO RUN AWAY?

Antonia is too young to run away. Though I don't doubt that she could pull it off.

But it doesn't really matter what I think. She's already far away.

SEPTEMBER 23

Peter sits me down at his pottery wheel, then makes his way effortlessly around it. With his hands held out in front of him he feels his way along the shelves for a bottle of Jameson and two small glasses. He backs up and sits on another stool.

I slide onto the seat, warm from his long daily labour. In my hands I roll a ball of clay, toss it from hand to hand, and then plop it down in the centre of the wheel head. My body has been hollowed out by worry, it saps my strength and makes my movements awkward. He holds out a cup. I catch it, and he pours whiskey over my clay-covered hands, *Stop, it's overflowing!* I bring it to my lips, the liquid flows and warms me all the way down my throat, running down my arm all the way to the wrist. Peter serves himself and places the bottle down at his feet. I soak my hands in the clay-dirtied water of a bowl set at my feet beside the wheel. I press down on the pedal, the wheel starts turning. I push both hands on the ball of clay, which reacts to my pressure like a cat slipping free of a caress. The blind man is my guide. *Keep your elbows on your knees and your knees against the wheel.* He drinks. *Knees ... against the wheel ... okay ...* I repeat after him, concentrating. He looks over in my direction, but not exactly, since he can't see me. *Shit!* I press too hard, the form is slipping away from me. I try to catch hold of it. He smiles to himself. *Ah, I see ... too fast.*

His studio is hung with photos that show a glorious past. Hairy naked bodies, hands in the earth or disappearing into the coats of gentle herd animals, and rivers and children. No idle hands. Each image is a room in a house that is home to a great many people who know no clear boundaries between inside and out: a fire, leaves, a stockpot, a yard full of creatures, a table – all the work of a life is captured in the movements of those who make it. I try to guess who that baby is, the one pictured still covered in slime on the belly of their tired-looking mother. No, not Antonia; she's a child from after, when something in this house had already shut its doors on the dissipated commune. Antonia was born as the desert encroached.

As I explore the images of this rich and carnal world, I recognize the potter. I take the picture down. There he sits, bare-chested before his wheel, both hands at work. Though he doesn't wear glasses, his expression is veiled. His sweet, wide-open smile breaks through any discomfort born of blindness, leaving no doubt that the man staring at us is in fact fully present. He's backlit. The surroundings aren't hard to imagine – most likely a yurt, or some other cloth shelter. To the left, behind him, you can see a large opening from a rolled-up strip of canvas. Thick rays of sun pour in. A woman stands beside him. She's caught in a strange movement, as if hugging herself against the cold by squeezing a lock of her long hair in each hand. Holding herself, she confronts the lens with an inexpressive face. I turn to Peter to ask, *Who's that?* But something in his sitting body, sad and overburdened, gives me pause. I keep my question to myself and take a second look at the photograph.

I can't tear my eyes from that face, like an opaque moon dividing the heart of the image. She is a silence in the dead centre of this effusion of life, in the play of the light that blurs the lines between inside and out. That is the space she occupies, exactly.

ANTONIA looks out an airplane window at
the ocean.

JOURNAL OF THE RUNAWAY

SEPTEMBER 25

The men here have beards and wear long robes, but not all, and I like how their flowing garments make every movement a bit like a dance. The narrow street presses them together in the evening light. There's something they're waiting for, some relief, you can feel it's on the way. Okay, I know what's coming because it's the same every night. While they wait for the exact time, they carve a path through the improvised market stalls, pastry stands serving fat crepes to break the fast — it's now, night has fallen. I blend into the crowd. I'm small, but oh those smells! Oh how they stir hunger in me. Sometimes someone hands me something. I take it without looking and scram. Tonight I turn off into the quieter streets near the market. A man is waiting to cross the street. Under his arm is a small package, something round wrapped up in paper. I imagine him going home with a sweet loaf for dinner. I join him in his appetite, staring longingly at this fat little loaf in its brown paper bag.

Nourish me, oh big fat loaf, fill me up, oh sweet soft loaf, let me devour you.

When the light turns green, I can't help but follow him. He takes his time, enjoying the golden hour. I lag behind, stay close to the shop windows, tie my shoes (though my laces weren't undone; it's part of my undercover pursuit). I am following a loaf. Exiled in this unfamiliar city, cut off from all protection and authority, I'm now living fully outside. The air rushes over me, every part of me mixes with everyone else's actions, and that turns me into something endlessly new. Sometimes I feel so confused and lonely it brings tears to my eyes. But tonight I'm focused on the bread man … when out of nowhere two shadowy men jump him, pull him toward a car and shove him in through the passenger door. The man cries out, fights back, and drops the bread. It rolls around at my feet. I fall to my knees, with both hands on the round loaf and my eyes glued to the man who is already gone in a practiced squealing of tires.

SEPTEMBER 27

I walk and walk and walk and walk.

I can feel the hot asphalt on my feet. I can feel the soles of my shoes sticking to the abnormally hot asphalt, as if the centre of the earth has risen up and is pushing at the surface, so close it might blow through at any moment. As if the earth were stretched taut like the skin of a drum, holding in the hot magma we might drown in. And here I am in the midst of this apocalypse, walking right through it, without a word, on the back of a boiling sea. I would love to just give up and dissolve, to be done with it all.

The air is a static cloud of gnats. Walking quickly, running really, is pretty much the only way to dodge their flightpath, which looks like nothing else, a thrumming belligerent suspension that seeps into eyes noses mouths ears, any opening at all. People are wearing masks for protection, or maybe they're the ones with TB. It's going around, they make the people who have it wear masks. Sometimes if I slow down I get stuck in one of those insect clouds and I feel like one more part of a living substance, no more no less.

I slow down and down and down until I'm going so slow I could fall.

I don't know this city but I love its light. It scorches everything, like ambient noise. Both press on you so tight you never feel alone. It's nothing like the vast sky by the St. Lawrence River at home, where I've disappeared time and again. Big skies like that don't give a damn about us little people.

Sometimes it gets too hot, times like today, so I take shelter.

In a book I read standing up in the aisle at the library but didn't finish because I was stressed out by the security guards with their obvious earpieces, I found a sentence that filled me with joy. I read it and it was so alive, so true, I could have run away and screamed. An energy came over me, and I reined it in with a laugh, standing up there with my grimy backpack at my feet, my carefully washed hands contrasting with my dirty wrists, and I laughed with a wordless joy:

'*In June the trees were bright dizzy green.*'

I put the book back on the shelf, reread the title on the spine and caressed each letter, to impress them in my memory. *T.H.E. M.E.M.B.E.R. O.F. T.H.E. W.E.D.D.I.N.G.*

Then I walked out, very carefully, so I wouldn't drop the ball of warmth that this sentence had produced in me, or the certainty that not all was lost, that there was still something left beyond the terrifying and fruitless rules people make and police enforce. Something that could ignore the rules, stare them down.

Behind me a stalky ageless security guard followed me through the library – one of those women who never retires, with her index and ring fingers pressed up on her earpiece and her head cocked back to more clearly hear her orders. She didn't even try to hide it. With her right hand behind her back she looked like a kid playing British Bulldog, ready to charge, but her joyless demeanour crushed any hope of play.

I'm sketchy and my backpack's too big and I must stink, and I move forward with a gentle smile, one step at a time, as if through some dense substance. The guard tailed me through the library but I just ignored her, such was my joy at *a bright dizzy green.*

Fall is in the air. It's warm and comforting. I get moving again, I am dispersed, dissolved in, and attentive to my surroundings.

I like hanging out around middle schools. I'll sit in the shade of one of the last surviving plane trees, watch the adults of tomorrow get an education. I listen to their yells, check out their walks. The girls have bodies like swelling buds and look worn out from this process of opening; the boys are wound tight, joints stretching as they flex muscles they didn't know they had. I try to read the promises these bodies make to one another, the directions they're pulled in, the future that preoccupies them. I try to guess how they might veer from the tracks their parents and teachers are trying to shunt them down. I scan the crowd in search of an uncertain movement, a body inhibited by complexes, that secret complicity shared by those who are forever out of place.

I never fit in at school. I held grudges against the others, though I liked them. Ever the good student, I got pressed into a mould and what got squeezed out took the form of a brick. So I picked it up and threw it. Far away from you. I'm sorry.

I catch a kind look from a man sweeping the sidewalk. He stops for a moment to look at me, not to take the weight and measure of my body as a series of parts, but to actually see me, yes me, on this bench.

THE YOUNG MAN sees her. Her hands lie
flat on her knees, hairy and sticky, they
are still yet alive as any garter snake,
doe, cat, fox, magpie, rabbit, shrew – a
whole crowd of watchful presences that
are with her. He sees her, sees them coming with her, from a mile away.

I sit still, unsure whether to flee or meet his gaze. I almost let myself go, because this one I could love. He has the controlled movements of those who get profiled wherever they go, know the cop car's back seat awaits at any moment. He spends his days outside, like me; he knows the streets. At night he takes off his fluorescent vest, has a smoke with his friends in front of the municipal garage, and then heads off with his bag slung over his shoulder. On his way home he walks through the city, sharp-eyed and nimble as a shepherd. His walk is at once slow and fast. Fast because he's speedy, slow because his every step is precise and well-defined. Each movement contains his entire trajectory.

I know all this because I followed him … One day I was afraid these crowds would swallow me up, to the point where I'd forget the letters to spell my own name. My first thought came from another book, that I'm being swallowed – *Avalée* … *O mon Québec.* Homesickness stopped me in my tracks, it stung like a slap in the face from an angered mother. A painful longing gripped me. I closed my eyes, and then he – the one I was following at a distance – did a little pirouette that lasted long enough for me slide back into his groove. In the lamplight I saw his face, it was banged-up but generous and open.

I haven't run away from everything, you know.

THE COLD SETS IN

She has taken down the photos from the potter's studio wall to better examine the land in the background and follow the community's expansion, step by step, the way you mark a child's growth with notches on a doorframe. The Girl With No Name first carefully numbered and marked out their place on the wall. She notices the same man in several photographs. He is lively, his hands always occupied – holding plants, in the earth, smoking. She plucks up the courage to ask Peter, *Who's that?*

'That's Gil. He could help us.'

When Gil comes, he'll be greeted by a precocious winter. Cold makes some substances evaporate, just as heat makes them heavier. Coats feel like paper over naked skin. In an attempt to warm himself, Gil tries to imagine the weight of a warm blanket, but tremors wrack his body, no comfort is forthcoming, no position tenable. Memories of Antonia the toddler in her comfy bed come rushing back – the joyful cries, the woolly babbling, the tiny adventures that perfectly simulated the secrets and scandals of adults, as children alone can vocalize. In his memory she was always going *Ohhh lalala doux doux lalalaaaaa*. And he would laugh without fully understanding.

Now this afternoon in the freezing-cold train compartment he isn't trying to find meaning in those faraway words. He focuses on the image. The thickness of the little one's blankets gives him pause. The idea of this visibly heavy fabric physically warms him. As in a dream, he relives how the child's body gives itself over completely, the chin perfectly tucked into the blanket's fabric, the feather-light pressure of tiny fingers on her chubby rolls. He slips away for a fraction of a second, and for a fraction of that time he is warmed; he sleeps, relaxes, gathers strength.

The next moment a bolt shoots through his body, like the lash of a whip through air stripped of all density; all density has evaporated, everything is reduced to the two dimensions of a drawing, the thinnest of lines against a pure white background. He imagines a white sheet of paper, his shock of red hair the sole trace of a third dimension in which his blood might circulate. His blood is mixed. He comes from Jackson, Tennessee.

'I'm dying,' he gasps.

This statement of fact appears in a speech bubble above his head; his agony is cut into panels, he's drifting up up and away from the South he has left behind. Yes, he may die, but his travels will go on, carried along by the train, indifferent, ever onward into the glacial air, galvanized by this fire that lightens it.

But he isn't dying. He's sleeping, badly. He'll make it to Montreal. He's in bad shape. But alive.

Friends of friends are waiting at the station. Over his numb shoulders and thin coat they throw another, thicker one. They button it up all the way to the neck, which they wrap in a scarf before topping his large head and wild hair with a fur cap.

The warmth puffs up his body, blood courses through his dilated vessels. He looks at them.

The group walks at a brisk pace. The human warmth of their meeting evaporates into a sky of a pitiless, one-dimensional blue. He now knows that unallayed flatness of implacable cold. He walks among them, matching their pace. He wants to take their hands, rejoin the world, but he doesn't want to unnerve them. He looks over at the woman to his right.

Her eyes puffy from crying all night, her face distraught. But still, something beautiful there: a deep care. He takes her hand.

He has taken her hand. They walk *hand in hand*.

The Girl With No Name is not relaxed. She doesn't know how to walk with the swinging of someone else's arms. She has always slipped lovers' holds: walking with a third hand in the back pockets of her jeans, walking with a third arm on her shoulder, breaking her neck. It's like carrying a branch still attached to its trunk. He has taken her hand and now the one thought that won't leave her in peace is that she won't be able to blow the snot already dripping down her nose onto her sleeve, because her other hand is also taken, carrying Gil's suitcase.

The two friends flanking this overhasty couple are caught in the churn of this clash, like a small craft buffeted by a big ship's wake. One slows down; the other pushes on.

She thinks of the *Empress of Ireland* that ran aground off Pointe-au-Père and the '*over one thousand people who lost their lives in the worst shipwreck in Canadian history.*' She doesn't think exactly in that way, like a book with a footnote recording the exact date of the disaster (May 29, 1914). But she does feel herself sinking in icy water. Or maybe that's just her runny nose.

She stops, puts down the suitcase, lets her left hand drop to fumble around in her pockets for a handkerchief. She locates one hiding in the bottom of her right pocket. It has grown so stiff from the cold she has to soften it up before putting her nose up to it.

His name is Gil and he comes from the 1970s, and those years will shed some light on Antonia's disappearance.

Now they drive through the cold. Their every movement is made in this cold, through this unreasonable cold. The Girl With No Name is white-knuckling the steering wheel of the van. She wants to talk. A small cloud of steam slips from her mouth.

'It's such a big area, and we're here stuck in this unreasonable frozen inhospitable land. All of us – animals, humans, machines – caught in the grip of the same cold. Does that make us a community? We've stopped bothering to make a world ... Is that what Antonia ran away from? The absence of a world?

The Girl With No Name's throat clenches and she stops talking.

DECEMBER 2

Since Antonia ran away, I've been haunted by images. Her abused body, stiff from the cold, lying in a ditch by the side of a frozen road. Her body abandoned, with nothing left to desire and nothing to flee and no one to meet.

I can't keep anything down except the alcohol I drink for warmth. Life has come unembodied, and in this forced abstraction I seek out direction.

Peter also hews close to his whiskey. His bottle has become an extension of his arm, a glass crutch. He doesn't drink to forget; he drinks to remember. He drinks to catch up with his epic, *My Antonia*.

We're in the Station kitchen. I make coffee. Gil hasn't taken off his coat or fur hat. He's blowing on his hands to warm them. The coffee starts percolating up, I place my hand above the element to be ready to interrupt the glugging at the right time, give the water enough time to rise up but not enough to boil again once it darkens.

I think of Mona. I think of us running through the fields. I think of Antonia, standing still before a tree while we were in its upper reaches, waiting, cheering her on. I think of Antonia standing so still I thought she too was rooted, like a tree. And her look as she scaled the trunk up to my eyes, and what I wanted to see there, shining with a power soon shaded by something I had not yet identified as determination but that scared me anyway. I jumped down from up in the tree, ashamed of my illusory elevation.

Antonia: I want to be with you. How can I be with you? I'll give up on everything that is not on your side. I'll be your beast of burden, carry whatever weighs on you.

FRAINETTI approaches the anemically pale
GIRL WITH NO NAME, who hasn't noticed the
coffee pot burbling. Frainetti leads her
to a chair, sits her down and briskly
rubs her cheeks and then gives her a
grandmotherly smooch on either cheek.

Frainetti is smiling.

DECEMBER 4

The cold sweeps down the moment the sun sets, as if a fridge door has been opened. Curling up in a ball is no longer enough to keep warm. I stole a few towels at the beach, and I use one as a pillow and the other two as blankets. I bundle them up every morning and sit on my bundle and think. Then something happened. It scared me at first. But I'm coming to accept that it might be good after all.

One day while I was packing up my camp under a bench, a woman came over and sat next to me. She was eating a croissant. Her sweater was covered in shiny crumbs. I stopped moving, hypnotized by her butter-shiny fingers, her golden crumbs, her discreet, polite chewing. When she had really and truly eaten the entire thing, she said something. I didn't answer; I listened. She had a heavy accent. Or maybe I'm just not used to being spoken to any more. She asked my name. I looked away. She told me about a part of town where the scrap-metal buyers (or fighters?) clustered. Up north. In this place there was shelter. And food. At the word 'food' I looked at her. The word hung throbbing in the air. I half-expected to see an apparition – chicken thighs, fat pastries, hot milk, or … anyway.

I liked her eyes. She brushed the crumbs off her chest and thighs and the bench. 'Crazy how much mess you can make with a single croissant! Okay, gotta go, but anyway,' she said, holding out a business card, 'here's the address, if you're interested.'

And she disappeared into the market crowd.

From that point on I think of her when I fall asleep at night, and I see her in my mind the second I wake up.

I haven't seen the croissant lady again, but the last three mornings in a row I've woken to find a paper bag next to my head. Pastries, still warm. I'm a light sleeper, in fact I am never really fully asleep, but I still haven't once caught her in the act. The first time, I spent all day wondering whether or not to taste it. Could it be poisoned? But one hungry night the bag's buttery stains wouldn't let me sleep, so I opened it up and wolfed down its entire contents. The slightly rancid taste of the butter, the dried yet oily substance of the three small pastries – it was wonderful.

That morning I pulled the croissant lady's card from my pocket. It was wrinkled and torn from my fumbling and hesitation. I flipped it over, and then over again. Just a name and location.

SCRAP METAL

PLATEAU DE LA CHORÉE

I carefully folded my towels and stuffed them in the bottom of my bag. And I was off.

In Place Jeanne-D'Arc there's a fountain. Turning the wheel gets the water running. It takes a few rotations before anything happens, then the water spurts out in big cold bursts that splash your feet. Even though I'm familiar with the fountain, it still gets me every time in the same way. First, you think that the water won't come this time, and that's when you get soaked by the sudden stream of water that you somehow weren't expecting. I figure it's a bit like life: you look around for it and stop believing in it and then *BANG*, there it is. But at the same time it's always there, without beginning or end.

I was reading in a different aisle in the library and I came across another sentence in a book by Marie Uguay. '*It was the beginning of the destructions.*' And now that idea is driving me crazy, just like the dizzy green from the *Wedding*. I didn't really realize it, but it threw me for a loop, in just the same way. It's the idea of the beginning and the end, back to back, and it strikes panic into my heart.

Antonia is visible from a distance,
through binoculars that cut the black
background into two circles.

The girl searches through her pack and
takes out a Ziploc bag. Inside is a
gloopy bar of soap. She picks it up and
places it on the cracked concrete rim
around the fountain drain. She unzips her
jacket, takes it off, and places it over
her backpack. She pulls off her sweater
too. Underneath she wears an unremarkable
T-shirt, with holes in it. She turns the
wheel. The water doesn't come the water
doesn't come the water doesn't come and
then, oh, there it is.

Whoooosshhhhh.

She splays her legs on either side of the
stream to avoid spraying her shoes. She
turns the handle hard, again. It turns and
turns, gathering momentum, and the water
surges out. She makes a steeple of her
hands and places it under the stream,
raises her hands to splash water on her
face. She takes the soap and carefully
washes her arms and neck. As the stream
tapers off, she turns the wheel again. She
rinses her hands, arms, and neck. Despite

her precautions, her T-shirt is now wet. The water has stopped flowing, the wheel is turning more slowly. She looks into the emptiness, as if lost in thought, leaning over to avoid splashing herself. She gives herself a shake and, as if she were awake again, takes off her T-shirt and puts it on her bag. She unties her shoes, takes off her socks, and places them on the drain. She unbuttons her jeans and pulls them down to her ankles, and throws them too on her heap of clothes. She also takes off her underwear and places it on top of her socks.

Antonia stands there, dripping like a mountain creek. Her chest is in between ages: budding breasts, visible ribs. A light emanates from her, cutting a space between the neutral, flattened air of this small place. She leans over and turns the handle one last time. She gets into it and washes her entire body.

Once I'm towelled off and my hair is brushed back and my nails scrubbed and my feet rubbed clean and my sandals dusted off, I get moving again. It's going to be a long walk from the Old Port to the city's upper reaches. You have to carve a path through the maze of alleys and a steep, treacherous no-man's-land to the mountainous plateau that breaks off into a cliff before the sea.

I still see no evidence of any camp, but I can hear the lookouts who form its mobile security perimeter. They are far-seeing, fast-acting. Their whistles cut through the air like tiny blades, a sound no bird could ever make, a warning pressed through their lips to let everyone know that a stranger is coming to camp. To whistle like that you have to curve your pointed tongue while keeping your cheeks stiff and pushing on the roof of your mouth. I can manage it only with my fingers or a blade of grass. How do they do it? Later on, they'll try to teach me, patiently laughing and occasionally sticking a finger in my mouth to position my tongue. But I'll never get it, it'll drive me crazy. People say it's genetic – your tongue can either do it or it can't. If you can't, your mother couldn't either.

I take my time. Take breaks to let the lookouts do their jobs. Sit down to eat. I pull a big handkerchief from my cloth bag and spread it on my knees, with the glass bottle I use for water and the paper bag with the last half-eaten pastry I saved from the day before.

A PARALLEL STATION

The abnormally stubborn cold never lets up. Bodies are exhausted from steeling themselves against it. Even machines struggle to keep running, their works cracking and straining in its icy death grip.

The Old Man is marshalling the troops. Wood has to be chopped every day, the pile is dwindling fast. The electricity flickers on and off as extreme frosts chisel away at the lines. The Group is losing power, much as they slip through the fingers of the Law, and this brings them a peace of sorts.

They aren't broadening the scope of their action or getting moving; they're stuck together, sheltering in place. Sometimes, driven by impatience or the need to challenge someone, Frainetti cries out: *'The investigation is stalling!'* It's stalling so badly its questions go deep, like a burn in the skin that penetrates down to the muscle and nerve, stopping only when it reaches unfeeling bone.

The policewoman is there too. If they're put off by her presence, they don't let on.

The days at the Station follow one upon the other, identical and insular. They spend their time doing what it takes to survive: stacking wood, storing provisions. The rhythm of the days seems to be set by the two men. Day is the kingdom of the Old Man; Gil reigns over the night. The policewoman, Mona, Frainetti, and the Girl With No Name establish other rhythms outside this domestic allocation of time. Frainetti spends a lot of time outside. Often the Girl With No Name comes with her, and sometimes Mona, who has pieced together snowsuits to protect them from the biting cold. The policewoman spends her time in bed with the Old Man, or looking after the two younger kids Mona has brought to the Station since her teenager left for the City. The policewoman teaches reading and math, Gil handles biology. When they aren't trudging around outside, the Girl With No Name and Frainetti shut themselves away in the back room for hours at a time, smoking like chimneys. One records the Group's actions for posterity, the other draws up plans.

Gil is on the night shift. He sits at the kitchen table, untying a handkerchief he has knotted on all four corners. But not until he has run the palm of his hand over the surface of the table, to brush off the last crumbs and make sure it's fully dry. He takes care over these preparations, to leave the others time to come to him, so they will be ready, tidily arranged like the Ziploc bags he sets out on the cloth. Each contains a handful of leaves or dried mushrooms. Now that the cold is deadly, he passes over his baggies of mushrooms. Going out for a trip in this cold could be fatal. Once Gil has bagged everything up, he sits in his chair like a poker player and waits for everyone to finish their jobs and sit down by his side.

The policewoman stays with them. As time goes on she finds her place. She wants to see where this story will end, wants to go where the law can't take her. She has come down off her high horse to walk the steep path down to them. She wears the smirk of those who are annoyed by humility, and the curves of her legs and torso are still reinforced by the gear she has never stopped wearing. They keep her in their sights, and she does the same, with no clear sense where this is going. But it works. Their relationship finds a balance in asymmetry.

DECEMBER 26

I'm in the shed chopping wood, and when I'm done I leave the axe stuck in a barely split log. I put on my coat and gather kindling in my long shirt. My toque is pulled down over my eyebrows. I go out into the short night that separates me from the Station, just long enough for the sweat on my back to freeze. I'd love to sit and gaze in wonder at the vast sky, but my nose and lips are already frosting over. I'm actually running by the time I shove the door open and cross the threshold into the Station. My eyes are still puffy at the thought of Antonia.

With the toes of my right foot I take off my left boot, and vice versa, and then I go into the kitchen to drop my load of firewood in front of the woodstove. The others are there, gathered around Gil, waiting for me. A moment passes as the stillness of this ritual fills me with rage. I want to grab a burning stick from the fire and burn their dry eyes. I breathe, instead I breathe.

Mona's sitting next to the potter, stroking his hand. She raises an arm to slide onto his knees, and kisses him, with tongue. Again and again she kisses him, suddenly and without regard for anything in the world save the urgency of kissing this man with her open mouth; nothing could be more urgent than winning his love with her hot tongue, licking his lips and sliding open his mouth and wrapping her tongue around his.

Gil's stories don't logically wrap the weft of space around the warp of time. I learn to take them as they come, stop trying to impose continuity. They tell of his wanderings, which never end but name new landscapes as they go. There are perpetual snowfields and deserts, plants and roaming animals (some dangerous), borders and caches and ruses as he wanders the length and breadth of an America of hinterlands and woodlands, outskirts and interzones, industrial wastelands and mountains and rivers and forests and other self-sufficient systems. Gil tells of his trips up and down the continent, deep down south, all the way to Mexico. He's a nomadic researcher, an anarchist botanist carrying the precious roots and herbs from which he extracts pure and refined drugs. He's the man who makes visions happen, and people pay him dearly. Many times over the years he has travelled to see Peter in Quebec, this land he fears, and many times also he has held Antonia in his arms, breathing in her skin and substance. He talks about her like an animal or spirit, and her shape shifts often in his stories.

We listen late into the night. Our eyes are red, the room a haze of different smoke and alcohol. The potter gives in to Mona's kisses. He slips his hands into the man's shirt she wears. It puffs up like a sail on her back, and when he can't grasp her shrunken breast he undoes the buttons, one at a time. He wants to suckle. And I want to join in, get between them like a child nesting in its parents' warmth. The Old Man rubs his face, out of fatigue or shyness, who knows. Gil observes us through the smoke, a strange bird, he's neither black nor white and his hair is a red shock. I scan the details of his face: freckles and keen eyes and full lips and large nose, skin grown leathery over the years, bristles of beard piercing through. I'll go join him in bed once the Old Man is asleep. The Old Man is leaning his neck back toward me, for a caress; he abandons its weight in his hand. *Dear man, oh your tenderness.*

I kiss his palms and walk with him to bed. I lay him down and tuck him in, caress his naked body under the sheet, caress the frayed sheet itself, and through it his plexus and stomach and thighs and the cock at the centre of his body, and slowly he reacts, a comical lump rises; I keep going, caress his thighs and his knees and his legs and his ankles and the two hills of his feet. He slides his hand under the sheet to stroke himself, picking up where I left off.

She folds up her towel and dries the corners of her mouth, brushes the crumbs off her shirt. In her bag she finds a small tobacco pouch. Pulls out a paper and skilfully rolls herself a smoke, baptizes it, pulls a lighter from her pocket. She lights it close to her face, shielding the flame, and the tobacco crackles as she inhales deeply and then exhales a big puff of smoke, gently upward and skyward, making a ring of her mouth. When she finishes, she crushes the butt on a stone and tosses it further down the trail. She gets up and contemplates the moon, sharply etched yet scarcely visible. In silence she looks out for signs that she is getting closer to her destination.

The whistling has stopped, message received. She gets walking again.

The rocky road soon turns into a steep path through a transitional area of shanties and housing projects. Stray dogs sometimes follow her for a while, sniffing away. Frightened, she picks up a stick for self-defence. But the dogs seem tame. Sometimes their masters summon them with a hiss from the shadows. They instantly recognize these sounds and go bounding back to their people. The houses are tiny and shabby and patched with scraps that flap and patter in the wind, a pealing of scattershot materials. Here and there a man or woman of uncertain age sits on a porch, watching her pass by. She says hello with an imperceptible smile and they answer in kind. It's relaxing.

After a long walk up – slender moon, her lengthening shadow, feet slipping on pebbles and frequent stops to catch her breath – Antonia emerges onto a barren yet surprising plateau.

Kids wheel around on bikes and headlights sweep the wide-open space. The ground is naked limestone, or shell sand, or maybe even sand-sand, though this is no beach.

She leans over, fingers a broken shell, picks it up and slips it into her pocket. The highway's embankment overlooks this expanse. Night has almost fallen. The horizon is alight with the last rays of day, which draw out the darkness, the evening's black light. Men are perched on the roof of a small dwelling whose tin sheeting snaps in the wind. They're nailing it down. These modest buildings look shakier than they are: in the fluctuating light of hanging bulbs and open fires and telephones, the wood-framed tarp walls appear to sway. But they hold.

She walks down a kind of street. There's a barber and a general store with a lit-up sign that says 'OPEN' in French and in Arabic. A convenience store doubling as a restaurant displays photos of African dishes on offer. Inside one tent she sees a young girl in a pool of light. She's listening to a man, and there's a younger man as well and they're laughing. The girl plasters her bangs to her forehead. Something he says makes her laugh, and she hides her face in her hands. He keeps his hood up. The sky is vast and cloudy. Antonia looks around, disoriented, sweeping the scene, gathering information.

Along her way she sees faces, momentarily lamplit and then plunged into darkness when a lamp flickers off. No one does anything to turn it back on or to otherwise lighten the sudden darkness. Other rays of light spring up here and there, illuminating other scenes and faces in the darkness, smiles that sparkle in the night. AutoTune music plays from a boom box. People are dressed like her, in cheap jackets and layers.

A man and woman dance to Middle Eastern music. Someone is filming with a phone; others gather around and clap their hands. Their movements are gentle, her smile tender, her fearlessness palpable, she dances with him as an equal partner.

For a long time Antonia stands still, watching them. The dancing makes her melancholy, she feels suddenly exhausted and lost, body heavy as lead. A red-eyed boy tells a story to a man who's dressed better than the others. She listens, amazed to find she understands. He says that whenever he goes into the LIDL he gets followed by police. He says they gassed him. The man asks where he's from. Afghanistan, Iran, Turkey, Bulgaria, Serbia, Austria, Germany, France – he might be forgetting somewhere. *French police?* he says in closing. *Tear gas and dogs.* Then she gets walking again.

This feels different than when she was completely alone. Something has changed. She's found a place of sorts. She's clumsy with her layers and bag, the accoutrements of a girl on her own on the street. She doesn't know on whose endorsement she is here. She doesn't know who is moving forward when she walks. But she also feels as if that might not matter, or maybe as if that might not matter *here*?

She's been noticed. The lookouts know their work. They have surrounded her as she makes her slow, uncertain, but steady approach. Their eyes are smiling, they see her. A man calls out to her, she turns her head toward him. He sticks his arm through the opening of a tarp in what looks like a makeshift restaurant, and holds out a shawarma, wrapped in paper. He talks to her, this time she doesn't understand but still reaches out to grasp the little package – it's nice and hot and the smell floors her, and she smiles at the man with every one of her teeth. Her smile makes the shawarma man laugh. He can see she's just a kid.

Now that she's arrived in the middle of this informal street, the centre of this hustle and bustle, she no longer knows which direction to walk in.

I HAVE NO IDEA WHERE I'M GOING EITHER

It's that ruthless hour in the middle of the afternoon when everyone has something to do. Not to be deterred, I undress; not to be deterred, I slip under the comforter that has seen a lot of comfort taken; not to be deterred, I plan to masturbate. *Getting into bed at this time of day is a political act.* Or so I say by way of justification.

My session is delicate, ladylike. When you apply yourself, it works. But the thing is, nothing dries you out quite like expectation. Sometimes nothing comes, no one cums. Like now. Time passes. I stay there listening to the sounds of the world. Out in the street it's the shouting of kids on their way home from school. The city is slowly but surely coming back to life, basking in the relaxation of those few hours communally authorized for non-work purposes. I'm waiting for a dealer who might sell me something, but what? I don't know, anything to take me away from here. Except there's no one here, in the silence of this bedroom. I hold on to this hope, on the edge of my bed.

I join the story *in media res*. I bring up the rear, like a magpie gleaning bits and pieces of heroic movements that came before, to cut and paste into this. I'm a woman in bed masturbating while the rest of the world is gainfully employed.

The worksite is not merely a worksite. The prison is not merely a prison. The two are inextricably linked.

The power station has to be dismantled. The migrants waiting for their cases to be assessed have to be parked somewhere. They are a new and renewable energy source, perfect for hazardous waste cleanup and other extractive projects. Remediating a nuclear site involves many steps. We do not lack work, we lack hands. You can't escape talk of the 'labour shortage' on the radio and in the newspapers. A scale not seen since the War and reconstruction. It's no longer clear whether we are in fact at war, or whether anywhere is at peace. But we confidently state that the Pilot Project under observation is successful. The cycle of workers is well-supplied, continuous, and stable. Costs are controlled, and economic sacrifices made. Once it has been proven, the innovative model will soon be implemented throughout the land. For now they are keeping a low profile. The work being performed in the camp is kept secret. With typical euphemism they speak of an 'industrial worksite.'

The land stretches out to the river, set back from the road. Its entry is poorly lit, its edges well-protected by barbed wire and police dogs.

The men and women are brought in on buses with tinted windows. The camp is divided into segregated barracks: a place to sleep, a place to wash. Midday meals are taken in small isolated groups in various different zones and confinement spaces on the site. The morning and evening meals are communal; families can sit together. Some of the women breastfeed before putting on their jumpsuits. A schoolbus picks children up at the barrack door to take them to the daycare at the other side of camp. They are kept busy while their parents go about their days. In the evening, after the workers have washed off in the decontaminating spaces, they go back to their barracks where the children join their mothers, and then in a crowd they set off for their assigned refectories, in alphabetical order. After the meal there is free time: they can walk to their quarters, spend time at the playground, swing on the swings, play ball. At 9 p.m. a siren blares to mark curfew. At 9:30, everyone has to be inside. There is a dispensary and an experimental medicine centre where they study the effect of radiation on the organism. The camp can accommodate 1,500 workers.

THE RUNAWAY HAS FOUND A COMMUNE

Antonia stands around in this strange camp on the plateau with a shawarma in her hand and a fire to warm her and the others. She doesn't know whether to approach, or rather how. And she's tired of this not knowing and she's tired of not having anyone here who knows her name or waits for her. She is suddenly weak, limp-legged, and all because of the shawarma. It opened a valve inside her. Since she started holding it in her hand, like a pouch of warmth, she's had the feeling that something else is going on.

For months now she's been inching forward, alone in the world. She's breaking up, it's a growth process. Rarely has she held something that brought her such comfort. Once or twice, perhaps, but never something quite as warm as this.

She stands there with the warm shawarma in hand. She holds it relatively high, and at a distance, as if not yet certain whether to accept it. It starts dripping, the meat juice dribbling down her wrist to be sponged up by her jacket cuff. She is standing, struck still, and although she's been walking for weeks, for months, she finds herself unable to put one foot in front of the other.

First her head: it won't stay still and starts bobbling around. Her shoulders slump and her knees bend, gently at first, but then before you know it she's crumpled on the ground like a pile of rags, shawarma still held tightly in her hand and in her line of sight. She looks at her strong, blackened, unyielding fingers. Still they grasp her little bundle tight, until it is pressed out of shape, the paper's creases less and less crisp, the bag sodden with grease-shiny meat juice.

Were the sea to rise up and overthrow her zodiac, still she would not let her pita go.

They're all around her now. A calm crowd has gathered, including the croissant lady, who is kneeling next to the dark mass that is the young girl's limp body on the ground. She gently pulls the backpack's straps to take it off, and together they carry the girl to shelter, and the shawarma as well.

Squatting in the woods, Frainetti watches the trucks come and go. It's late in the day. Things are winding down. The guys at the worksite have a final smoke and then pick up their massive lunchboxes. They sit on the barrack front steps, take off their steel-toe boots and put on running shoes as light as slippers.

Though she is cold, Frainetti can't stand up and stretch her legs. The humid air forms a halo around the big work lights placed at regular intervals along the meticulously barbed-wired perimeter. All that's missing is a watchtower in the middle, perhaps a floodlight sweeping the black night for escapees. She must be dreaming. She wants to spit, but her mouth is dry.

A bus drives up to the gate, the last of the day. Its tinted windows don't let her see inside. All Frainetti can see is the driver's arm reaching out the window to the checkpoint, to pass him a form. A moment passes, then the guard gets out and walks over to the bus door. The driver opens it for him. Ten minutes pass. The guard gets out again. His face is an empty book; his face is a filing cabinet a table a desk lamp, not a face one could imagine kissing. The bus starts and disappears behind the camp barracks.

Frainetti is freezing. She makes her way back. First she walks a ways to find her bike where she hid it in the ferns, and then she rides back to the station. The Girl With No Name is waiting for her on the porch. She's wearing her winter suit, a patchwork of snared rabbit skins, and she's worried.

FEBRUARY 15

It takes careful planning to commit an act of sabotage. I'm struggling to convince myself that it's necessary, paralyzed by thoughts of *What difference will it make anyway?* When we first moved into the Station, we often gathered for discussions around the kitchen table, our heads warmed by the hanging lamp. This constant back-and-forth fed our sense of what defined us as a group. It was more than just a way to know whose strengths could be counted on. It was a way to adduce first principles, since no thought formulates itself and no truth is self-evident, like a pitcher of water on a table. Our group wants to combat a certain world order, and that means confronting power and its representatives. And we must do this with our heads, and we must also do this with our bodies.

Recently it feels like we've stopped seeing. As if we can no longer look deeply enough into ourselves to sit together at the table, under the kitchen light, working to share and shore up our visions. Something is slipping away, though what that something is we can't easily name.

Fear has charged back in, beginning its expropriations. It cracks its whip, and toxic terrors flood in. I try to regain my footing, but the world has reverted to its former state, again subject to the rule of fear.

FRAINETTI UNROLLS A MAP

We clear up after supper. Frainetti eyes the policewoman. *I don't know if I can trust you,* says her look. *But I guess I don't really care.* The policewoman is impassive. *Just trust me, girl.*

Frainetti hesitates at first, and then takes a rolled-up paper from her bag and proceeds to unroll it. It's a map. She holds out her arm. *Pass me those books, okay?* The policewoman grabs four books off a shelf and hands them to Frainetti, who puts one on each corner of the map. *There. The worksite is actually a camp.*

FEBRUARY 29

Something in the earth's curve sends us rolling toward one another – unless some other force of attraction is at work. We may not be on the same plane, but our meeting seems preordained by her fraught relationship with Order. She's trying to gain power by upholding it; I want to find its cracks and watch it crumble. She at once attracts and repels me.

Her presence is a test, each result a false positive. When she looks at you your heart and vision blur, you think she thinks you want her and you're scared that you might want her because wanting her would be an aberration. We're chasing our tails, or licking them, and that's no help when you're trying to see clearly.

We put up with the policewoman for the Old Man's sake. He lets her in. She sleeps in his bed. The station has become her home. He takes off her uniform, unbuttons her shirt, undoes the button of her awful polyester pants. He unlaces her shoes, shoes so ugly they smother everything like greasy cardboard, shoes that have no truck with grace, that represent the basest form of Order, shoes clearly not cut from the leather of any earthly creature. He takes them off her the moment she crosses the Station's threshold, not in the manner of a slave subjected to their master's routine, but like a loving teacher, establishing the terms of disarmament.

I'm not disgusted, but I should at least be afraid. There's something terrifying in their love. No good can come from the union of cop and hunter, right? Two creatures whose vocation is capture, two trackers, one nightstick. I'm haunted by images of beaten people. And I live with them, sleep with them. Little by little I get used to living in this precarious balance, accustomed to the substance of our strange habits.

MARCH 2

No blame

The group is at a standstill. Gil showed up and nothing happened. No one has gone out looking for Antonia. I've stopped calling hospitals; even Peter the potter is drinking less. We're still here at the Station, we're still trying to produce some new substance, but we've misplaced sight of what it is. As if we've lost our sheet music and are suddenly all playing by ear. In fact, we've stopped working altogether. Our habits remain, like glue holding our actions together. They cover up the void of waiting the way a carpeting of boughs conceals a trap in the forest.

What are we feeling? It's hard to pin down. Profound lassitude, pervasive numbness, the sense that the very thing that formerly uplifted us has grown heavy as lead. As if something has receded, like a wave that will never come back, and has left in its wake a rocky, dry shoreline. With Frainetti here we can at least feel that something is being cooked up anyway.

Tonight we'll put off going to bed, suck on old candies, and sip on mulled wine. Frainetti has begun telling a story. It's 'The Emperor's New Clothes.'

'What? You don't know that one? Ha!'

Embarrassed looks all around. Mona clicks her tongue. 'You didn't know we were a bunch of yahoos? Quit looking at us like that and tell your story.'

Frainetti focuses, looks at the ceiling. 'Okay, okay.' She clears her throat and settles herself on her chair.

'Once upon a time,' she begins, 'there was a king. Or an emperor? I can't remember. Who cares? He was very, what's the word, *orgoglioso*. Proud. And vain – ooh la la, so vain! Always looking for new clothes, better and better clothes, that one. Every week he had to have a new suit. The palace tailors would start working. They'd drive themselves crazy, trying to lay at his feet the most beautiful garments in the land. One day, it was a suit dark as a night pierced with starry diamonds. Next week, another suit, azure, a bottomless blue with a moiré pattern, you would swear that the clouds themselves were sewn into the fabric. Another outfit was fluid as water, made of raw silk from an unknown country where monks raise silk-worms in cocoons spun from gold.

'When the king received these treasures, he was thrilled – for a while. His joy was intense but fleeting, his dissatisfaction already lurking, like ash waiting to tarnish his jewels. He would walk away unhappy, then he'd stroll the palace hallways with puffy eyes, wearing his terry-cloth bathrobe and old slippers. No, nothing was ever good enough for His Highness.

'One day, one of the helpers went to see the Head Tailor, who was on the verge of burnout. He was head-down on his worktable, surrounded by little mounds of stimulants, hiding the eyes he could barely keep open behind dark glasses. She's one of those people who just can't keep her mouth shut. She walks over to the slumped couturier. She has an idea.

'"C'mon, let's make him a naked suit. We'll just work on the words and the movements to present it. Make it clear that this suit is invisible to rubes and yokels, they're just not sophisticated enough to see it. He won't be disappointed. He'll finally get the new clothes he's been dreaming of. Because that's all they are: a dream!"

'The Tailor sent this impertinent girl away. But later, at a loss for new ideas, he called her back. He listened to her again, then called in his whole team to explain the little bit of theatre they would have to put on.

'"So the suit will be … nothing! We'll give the King a handful of wind, and he'll put it on, knowing he can't not like it, because it doesn't exist. We have to be perfect, though. No one screw this up! If even one person doesn't believe in this, it will be our undoing!"

'All night the armies of errand-boys went through the motions of delivering cloth, and the Tailor observed them, interjecting from time to time.

'"No, no, no – that will never do! Never do! What is this potato sacking you would have me put at the King's feet? You want to see us all hanging from the gallows? No no and *no*! Off with you, and find me something new!"

'And then the morning of the procession was here at last. At the head of the procession was the young girl, singing the praises of the clothing, shaking up the magic potion, enchanting the public with the notes of a miraculous ritornello.'

Frainetti pauses, holds out a glass, and pours more wine.

'And then what? Did it work?' someone asks.

'I can't believe that you've never heard that one before!' answers Frainetti, stretching.

I AM MADE OF STUBBORN STUFF

I sit here as my ass gets sore on the deflated cushion of my stubbornness. I'm looking inward, pale and unkempt, no longer party to the seductions unfolding on this strip of land I at first thought was vacant but now know is teeming with people. I'm not alone here, and I'm not the first one to make my way through it.

The beginnings of a form taking shape, small accumulating like mineral sponges. I see movements, subtle but constant, and feel the soft ground at my feet. And if I list what I find here it will fit in the bag that was already there and now carries the rest of my things: a leaf a shell a scarf a bottle a pot a knife. That's all.

NIGHT FALLS AND SO DO OUR BODIES

I split a log with a clean *chop*. As I limb this tree that I cut down last summer I can still hear the chainsaw's roar, feel the motor's hot exhilarating chugging, which makes me want a hard veiny cock and gets me soft and wet.

I can function on three hours sleep a night. I can wake up to soothe a feverish child, and I can drink all night and still have the kids' lunches ready in time for school and drive along the endless dusty roads without batting an eye. All these things are hard, but I can do them. And yet I find myself a little too soft when the time comes to stand for the Revolution.

In town, people are talking. Cars slow as they drive by the Station. Drivers and passengers shoot us belligerent looks. If it wasn't so cold, they'd roll down their windows and spit.

To spit is to commit a violent act, like slapping a face without raising a finger. *Cccrruuugh, chrachiit.* To spit cuts an unbridgeable chasm between two worlds that it alone can cross, and only for the sake of an insult.

Mona comes out with a long whip and cracks it on the road. She's chasing off the cars that slow to a crawl as they roll by the Station again and again. The whip makes a harsh slap on the hoods and roofs. She yells, *Whatcha want? Can't you see the shell has run dry? The lines are empty. NO MORE GAS!*

When the next car comes, she starts again. She's had the time to light a smoke, the pack in the pocket of her jumpsuit forms a little square bump on her heart that just might block a bullet if someone came after her.

C'mon out and walk on your own two feet. Thwak! We're gonna get you up on your hind legs, or else back to the doghouse.

Thwak! Show me what you got! Everything that keeps you down, everything that won't let you break free. So tight it keeps you fake-hard, like a cock ring. Or what … Another boring-ass barbecue, on that lawn that isn't even green since you can't water anymore? Sitting around your illegal hot tub? Sure you can still climb in, it's nice and warm. But who'll feel your tits? You may as well drown in your fucking hot tub, with your remote-control ozone and river view. What's the difference? Can't you see it doesn't matter anymore? You feel the need for other people's envy. Nothing else still gets you hard, hey? It's been so long since you could tap one of your neighbours at the end of the night, lick her gaping ass in the foamy water of your hot tub, your hard dick waiting its turn in the churn.

And what'd you think your wife was doing all that time? Do you know? Did you ever even wonder? *Do you really think she was sleeping peacefully in her big waterbed, drowning in a pile of puffy pillows big enough to throttle a litter of kittens. You really thought she was* waiting for you?

Cruaghgggh! It's Mona's turn to spit now.

Eventually the cars tire of this. But they'll be back. Frainetti comes back for dinner with stories about what they're accusing us of. They're saying we're smuggling people out of the camp, preparing attacks, eating cats. Her laugh rings out a while before an embarrassed silence descends on the group. *If only.*

JOURNAL OF THE GIRL WITH NO NAME

MARCH 8

One day when the cold is less intransigent I work on the porch, caulking around the old windows. Concentrating on small, minor things eases my stress and helps me get a grip on my life, or maybe helps my life get a grip on me. I sense a car behind my back, driving slowly. Though I'm still focused on my work, some part of me listens to this car as it drives by, slows down – it's slowing down more than it should. The stop sign is quite far up the road, and no one ever stops here except to insult us. We're used to it. So I'm on my guard as I lay down a bead of this malleable white substance. I hear the car stop and a dull thud, followed by a slamming door and then tires peeling out and a motor revving. I turn around with my caulking gun drawn in self-defence and see the red tail lights recede into the distance and disappear around the bend. I look at the dark mass the car dropped on the road. I leap down the stairs and run over, my heart is aflutter, my throat constricted, but my head, my head already knows.

I lean over the small inert mass on the blacktop. I can't see well. I touch it. Try to register breathing – success! It's weak, but I feel it. I yell out. I cry out to the Station, the Old Man, Frainetti, *Gil!* The policewoman comes out first. She's red-faced and dishevelled and her clothes have been thrown on in haste. She leans over Mona. I tell her to '*Get the others! And a mattress to carry her.*'

I stay at Mona's side that night: Mona who's impossible; Mona who isn't dead.

Mona had her first kid very young, but you'll never hear her say *too young*. She accommodated her child as a pure offshoot of herself, not acting without love but without thinking or talking about it to anyone. She didn't ask questions about motherhood; she invented it anew, for herself and her son, a motherhood made for them alone. When she'd get bored she'd strap her infant to her back and they'd set out into the woods. They would go out walking for hours on end, stopping in the sun or on a big flat warm rock to rest a little. She would snack on whatever they turned up in their travels, and when he got hungry she gave him her breast, then went looking for something to drink.

Even then she was drinking a lot. I asked her about it once, and her answer was clear. *I've always drunk. I've always drunk as much as I could soak up.*

She was born on the family farm in Précieux-Sang, a farm she still lives on, rundown and fallow, with no other living soul but her and her dogs and the men who pass through, her and the children she has had over the years, the ones she kept.

I see her laid out on the asphalt, emaciated body tanned brown, hair matted and glued to her skull, where the blood flowed I guess, or so it looks in the night that makes it a less shocking picture. I look at this woman, so frail yet so strong and possessed of a mineral force that makes her stand out, a harsh unsettling presence. But I also see a strength one can surrender to, take shelter and find comfort in.

Mona's integrity is rooted in the ageless knowledge of a world that exists to be lived in. Her movements are true and precise. She knows how to feed the hungry and care for the sick; she'll figure out a way to survive.

A few years ago, I changed my life. This change could not have been more radical or more commonplace. I moved out, broke up the family home.

To survive this great sorrow, and to protect it from being shredded by the legal and social systems lined up to file it safely away, I adopted a political stance toward love and sexuality. Not a formal position or academic exercise, but a practical approach. It was minor, honest, far-reaching; it transformed me.

I walked a lot in those days. I stared up at the vast city sky. I felt the road's hot asphalt and the nip of fall in the air. My daily needs had me travelling great distances through the city in search of the best substances at the best prices. I don't want to say *cheapest*, that would imply disdain and not reflect my gratitude for the secondary economy that saved me. In a church basement I found dishes, in the affluent western suburbs there were clothes for my daughter, and at the Salvation Army by my house a quilt and a new coat to replace mine that had grown threadbare. The community centre had bulk chickpeas. Everything was rough to the touch, nothing fancy for sure, but every object came with stories, other people's stories that would now enter into my own.

Along with my sadness was some sort of powerful momentum I wanted to share. I was a fugitive who refused to be pigeonholed into the regular slots, in love or in work. I figured there must be some way to live like a disappeared person, outrun the rules, carve out a free space right in the middle of all this: streets, city, sky, trees, river, train tracks, tall grass. To be right in the thick of it, integrity intact.

I fell a lot that summer. One time I had to be carried. We were walking with a dog that had, just that morning, killed another, smaller dog. He must have just wanted to play. Before anyone knew what had happened, the smaller one's head lay crushed in the larger one's jaw. We were walking together, okay not me, I was sitting in the stretcher formed by the interlaced arms of my friend and the murderous dog's mistress. In this manner we made our way to the forest, searching for a river. The animal looked despondent, and so did its master, who didn't know what to make of her love for an animal that had killed another. 'You killer!' were her astonished words for the creature she had trained, cared for, and loved.

I knew no way of thinking that might help her, while the dog walked along beside us, looking at once regretful and oblivious to the cause of all this trouble. All I wanted was to embrace a life that did not mean wholesale resignation. I would be powerful and vulnerable, and definitely precarious.

THE TRIAL

The Accused sits naked in her box. This is no figure of speech: she is concealed only by her long loose hair, which slightly warms her and covers her breasts and her stomach, like long grasses. She is watching, watching herself produce this excess of heat. *Self-sufficient* is an odd thing to be thinking at this moment, when she has been stripped of everything so she may no longer serve for anything.

CROWD: Cover her up! Not even witches went naked to the stake.

JUDGE: You must know that, where you now stand, there can be no pardon and no redemption. That's why you stand naked before us. But we're here to listen. What do you have to say in your defence?

The judge's flinty stare straightens her up. She looks him over – the weave of his robe, his skin pockmarked and florid from drinks at the club – and she sees what his lofty position can't hide. She sits up straight and pulls the police officer's arm as far as the handcuff will allow. The chain sits like a hyphen between them, but leaning like an acute accent.

She stands up and tugs on the arm of the police officer, who also has to stand up to approach her, releasing the tension between their bodies. She catches the judge's eye and, here in the halls of justice, transmutes his attention into a microphone. She clears her throat, takes a deep breath, and starts to sing. It starts out thin, off-key, but then the tension squeezes out her song like a billow. Her listeners' throats clench tight. Her song is familiar yet transformed, a song that should have remained secret, a call to summon birds, a secret song that would make the coyote lie down with the wolf, and the grizzly with the polar bear. A mutant music, unstable, untethered to any tradition, it mixes snatches of refrains that loop back around but never die out, just sweep us up in their flow.

It's never easy to start dancing cold, and it's hard to dance handcuffed to a policewoman. The woman in uniform can read the thoughts of the woman with no clothes and moves to set her free. From her right pocket the policewoman pulls the key ring containing her every order. From the middle, she selects the key that binds her and inserts it into the poor-quality lock that encloses the wrist, the same cheap lock as on the diaries in which young girls consign their lives, insubstantial writings they yet wish to conceal. Because these belong to them, or because by concealing them they make it so. The naked woman watches as the key penetrates the crenelated passage of the lock, the hand turns, the mechanism springs, and the quiet sound of the handcuff's jaw relaxing can be heard. Her wrist is rubbed by the other hand which has never ceased to be free. The policewoman leans over toward her ear and makes a wish, provocative: *C'mon, girl, dance now!*

PLEADINGS OF THE ACCUSED

'I am all the captured ones, put on display, and this place is worse than any desert. But I still fully intend to dance; just watch me!

'I see you, Judge who still doesn't see what's going on but is thrown off by it all. I'm naked, my breasts are shaking, and my lustful eyes betray a sinister intent. All that is working against

you, Your Honour! So I stretch my arms and legs a little, and I dance around in this narrow box for the accused.

'I draw a circle of protection, and inside it I find balance. I kick up the wind of sad, disillusioned keyboards. There is no one to laugh, believe me, the circle that protects me is my charm, and it travels with me.'

The judge is hearing this music for the first time, and not invoking his authority to put a stop to it; it is the evidence he has been waiting for. He feels the music in his body, he grows stiffer with each kick of the drum, relaxes when the harp comes in, and that funny flute that might be a synthesizer. He hears the singing voices now, deep and inarticulate. The judge is them, the judge is playing the violin, the judge is on cymbals, on that funny flute, as if all in unison were singing the theme song of The Law. But no one is moving any more. He's listening with his entire being, knows that he won't hear any more. His body stiffens, and so does his cock.

'I know,' says the Accused, *'I know I make you hard, and I will also make you last. Your cock is the gallows on which to hang the many you kill because you could not fuck them. I want to cry out:* Don't you hear my heart pumping and flowing? *But it's too late for desire and declarations. I'll take the snares over the gallows.*

'I'm focusing so I too can attain a climax, spread my legs a little and back up to rest on the railing whose wood gleams with the polish of generations of despair. I rub this warm wood with my cunt, which is the opposite of hard; I rub it off and wet the wood as if it could bear flowers again, as if all the captives could in this way go back in time to before when they were captured.'

The music doesn't last forever, the waves make a curve that the room must come down from, it's inexorable. The music stops. The wood is hard again, the judge's eyes once more heavily lidded.

She lowers her arms, the circle disappears, she sits back down on the bench, frozen with terror.

She is delivered unto them.

The policewoman has now been replaced by another, whose closed-book face is a thin veneer over an insult. There will be no laughing on her watch. She pulls the accused's wrist to fasten the same handcuffs again. *Clack, thud. Clack clack clack* go the teeth of the lock. Her entire body is seized by one last tremor, her breathing deserts her, she is carried, covered with a shroud because she's dead. The song and dance were her sad nuptials. Sorrow is our path, our lives and deaths intermingled.

The nurse has been working since the previous day. She'll make it, sure, but five a.m. is tough. The first rays of daylight bring everyone back to their duties, including the duty of being in pain.

She feels the rush of adrenaline. Even the most vulnerable patients have made it through the night. The second she lowers her guard, fatigue seizes her. It's visible everywhere, her colleagues' faces and the eye wrinkles and their waxy complexions. She tries to smile but something inside her is tenser than usual. Today she feels that her spirit might leave her body at any moment. She looks at things and people as foreign objects, even her hands have become things she has no real control over, just flotsam swept up by the sea. She snorts and gives her head a shake. She's fighting off the numbness and the threat of the abyss that comes with it.

Intensive Care is no longer fully safe, she can feel it. Like an animal on the prowl, she lifts her nose to read the direction of the wind, unravel its texture and the dangers it contains. Her gown is made of a fabric whose soft drape is stiffer at the armpits, where the cold sweat runs when procedures go badly. Her uniform is on the big side. Especially lately, though it's not her garments stretching. She still tries to find herself sexy when she puts on clean scrubs at the start of every shift, tries to get back to the joys of the early days, playing out the fantasy of the nurse naked under her uniform. Even masturbating to the thought of erotic positions on shining metal stretchers has become a chore. Fantasies don't hold up to the realities of work.

It's the end of her shift, and she feels like a beer, is contemplating leaving when they send her someone over from Emergency. A strange bird. She is swimming in that gown, worse even than the nurse. She sizes up the sheet-white creature, for whom this may well be the end of the road – but something grabs her in this patient's burning-hot breath. There is life, beating there, just enough to survive. There's a stubbornness.

By 6:30 the frail body has been hooked up to the machines. The respiratory therapist and patient attendant have moved on to other bedsides. The nurse stays a moment longer to watch the woman who smells like fire, her body working, chest rising and falling, the silent but effective intelligence running through veins that are still holding on, that are holding fast. There's something about this life on the chasm's edge, the coexistence of strength and refusal to abdicate. She looks into it like a terrifying, uplifting mirror. And she lifts up this mirror image, and then tosses the garments of her exhaustion in the big laundry bag on her way out.

ABOUT THE AUTHOR AND TRANSLATOR

Anne Lardeux was raised in France and lives and works in Montreal, where she painstakingly follows her ideas and convictions where they lead. Her multidisciplinary practice spans music, film, and writing, and is not easily separable from her social activism and caring work. Together they constitute an unsparingly honest but playful interrogation of how we live that turns up glimmers of hope in unlikely places. *The Second Substance* (*Les mauvais plis*) is her first novel.

Pablo Strauss's translations for Coach House Books include *Fauna*, *The Supreme Orchestra*, and *Baloney*. He is a three-time finalist for the Governor General's Literary Award for translation, for *The Country Will Bring Us No Peace* (2020), *Synapses* (2019), and *The Longest Year* (2017). Pablo grew up in Victoria, B.C., and has lived in Quebec City for fifteen years.

Typeset in Adobe Jenson Pro and Manuka.

Printed at the Coach House on bpNichol Lane in Toronto, Ontario, on
Zephyr Antique Laid paper, which was manufactured, acid-free, in Saint-
Jérôme, Quebec, from second-growth forests. This book was printed with
vegetable-based ink on a 1973 Heidelberg KORD offset litho press. Its pages
were folded on a Baumfolder, gathered by hand, bound on a Sulby Auto-
Minabinda, and trimmed on a Polar single-knife cutter.

Coach House is on the traditional territory of many nations, including the
Mississaugas of the Credit, the Anishnabeg, the Chippewa, the Haudeno-
saunee, and the Wendat peoples, and is now home to many diverse First
Nations, Inuit, and Métis peoples. We acknowledge that Toronto is covered
by Treaty 13 with the Mississaugas of the Credit. We are grateful to live
and work on this land.

Edited by Alana Wilcox and Caitlin O'Neil
Cover design by Natalie Olsen, Kisscut Design
Interior design by Crystal Sikma

Coach House Books
80 bpNichol Lane
Toronto ON M5S 3J4
Canada

416 979 2217
800 367 6360

mail@chbooks.com
www.chbooks.com